In the Cage

by
Henry James

A Classic
&
A Sequel

At Chalk Farm

by
Mary F. Burns

Word by Word
Press

Copyright ©2019 by Mary F. Burns
Published by Word by Word Publishing
San Francisco, California

ISBN: 9781092202930 (for *At Chalk Farm*)

"In the Cage" by Henry James is a work in the public domain, and is reprinted here with no copyright or other claims.

"At Chalk Farm": All Rights Reserved. Printed in the United States of America. Permission is given for brief quotations for critical articles and reviews.

Cover Art: *Winter Afternoon, Chalk Farm* (1935) by Geoffrey Rhoades

❧

In the Cage

by

Henry James

CHAPTER I

It had occurred to her early that in her position—that of a young person spending, in framed and wired confinement, the life of a guinea-pig or a magpie—she should know a great many persons without their recognising the acquaintance. That made it an emotion the more lively—though singularly rare and always, even then, with opportunity still very much smothered—to see any one come in whom she knew outside, as she called it, any one who could add anything to the meanness of her function. Her function was to sit there with two young men—the other telegraphist and the counter-clerk; to mind the "sounder," which was always going, to dole out stamps and postal-orders, weigh letters, answer stupid questions, give difficult change and, more than anything else, count words as numberless as the sands of the sea, the words of the telegrams thrust, from morning to night, through the gap left in the high lattice, across the encumbered shelf that her forearm ached with rubbing. This transparent screen fenced out or fenced in, according to the side of the narrow counter on which the human lot was cast, the duskiest corner of a shop pervaded not a little, in winter, by the poison of perpetual gas, and at all times by the presence of hams, cheese, dried fish, soap, varnish, paraffin and other solids and fluids that she came to know perfectly by their smells without consenting to know them by their names.

The barrier that divided the little post-and-telegraph-office from the grocery was a frail structure of wood and wire; but the social, the professional separation was a gulf that fortune, by a stroke quite remarkable, had spared her the necessity of contributing at all publicly to bridge. When Mr. Cocker's young men stepped over from behind the other counter to change a five-pound note—and Mr. Cocker's situation, with the cream of the "Court Guide" and the dearest furnished apartments, Simpkin's, Ladle's, Thrupp's, just round the corner, was so select that his place was quite pervaded by the crisp rustle of these emblems—she pushed out the sovereigns as if the applicant were no more to her than one of the momentary, the practically featureless, appearances in the great procession; and this perhaps all the more from the very fact of the connexion (only recognised outside indeed) to which she had lent herself with ridiculous inconsequence. She recognised the others the less because she had at last so unreservedly, so irredeemably, recognised Mr. Mudge. However that might be, she was a little ashamed of having to admit to herself that Mr. Mudge's removal to a higher sphere—to a more commanding position, that is, though to a much lower neighbourhood—would have been described still better as a luxury than as the mere simplification, the corrected awkwardness, that she contented herself with calling it. He had at any rate ceased to be all day long in her eyes, and this left something a little fresh for them to rest on of a Sunday. During the three months of his happy survival at Cocker's after her consent to their engagement she had often asked herself what it was marriage would be able to add to a familiarity that seemed already to have scraped the platter so clean. Opposite there, behind the counter of which his superior stature, his whiter apron, his more clustering curls and more present, too present, h's had been for a couple of years the principal ornament, he had moved to and fro before her as on the small sanded floor of their contracted future. She was conscious now of the improvement of not having to take her present and her future at once. They were about as much as she could manage when taken separate.

She had, none the less, to give her mind steadily to what Mr. Mudge had again written her about, the idea of her applying for a transfer to an office quite similar—she couldn't yet hope for a place in a bigger—under the very roof where he was foreman, so that, dangled before her every minute of the day, he should see her, as he called it, "hourly," and in a part, the far N.W. district, where, with her mother, she would save on their two rooms alone nearly three shillings. It would be far from dazzling to exchange Mayfair for Chalk Farm, and it wore upon her much that he could never drop a subject; still, it didn't wear as things had worn, the worries of the early times of their great misery, her own, her mother's and her elder sister's—the last of whom had succumbed to all but absolute want when, as conscious and incredulous ladies, suddenly bereft, betrayed, overwhelmed, they had slipped faster and faster down the steep slope at the bottom of which she alone had rebounded. Her mother had never rebounded any more at the bottom than on the way; had only rumbled and grumbled down and down, making, in respect of caps, topics and "habits," no effort whatever—which simply meant smelling much of the time of whiskey.

CHAPTER II

It was always rather quiet at Cocker's while the contingent from Ladle's and Thrupp's and all the other great places were at luncheon, or, as the young men used vulgarly to say, while the animals were feeding. She had forty minutes in advance of this to go home for her own dinner; and when she came back and one of the young men took his turn there was often half an hour during which she could pull out a bit of work or a book—a book from the place where she borrowed novels, very greasy, in fine print and all about fine folks, at a ha'penny a day. This sacred pause was one of the numerous ways in which the establishment kept its finger on the pulse of fashion and fell into the rhythm of the larger life. It had something to do, one day, with the particular flare of importance of an arriving customer, a lady whose meals were apparently irregular, yet whom she was destined, she afterwards found, not to forget. The girl was blasée; nothing could belong more, as she perfectly knew, to the intense publicity of her profession; but she had a whimsical mind and wonderful nerves; she was subject, in short, to sudden flickers of antipathy and sympathy, red gleams in the grey, fitful needs to notice and to "care," odd caprices of curiosity. She had a friend who had invented a new career for women—that of being in and out of people's houses to look after the flowers. Mrs. Jordan had a manner of her own of sounding this allusion; "the flowers," on her lips, were, in fantastic places, in happy homes, as usual as the coals or the daily papers. She took charge of them, at any rate, in all the rooms, at so much a month, and people were quickly finding out what it was to make over this strange burden of the pampered to the widow of a clergyman. The widow, on her side, dilating on the initiations thus opened up to her, had been splendid to her young friend, over the way she was made free of the greatest houses—the way, especially when she did the dinner-tables, set out so often for twenty, she felt that a single step more would transform her whole social position. On its being asked of her then if she circulated only in a sort of tropical solitude, with the upper servants for picturesque natives, and on her having to assent to this glance at her limitations, she had found a reply to the girl's invidious question. "You've no imagination, my dear!"—that was because a door more than half open to the higher life couldn't be called anything but a thin partition. Mrs. Jordan's imagination quite did away with the thickness.

Our young lady had not taken up the charge, had dealt with it good-humouredly, just because she knew so well what to think of it. It was at once one of her most cherished complaints and most secret supports that people didn't understand her, and it was accordingly a matter of indifference to her that Mrs. Jordan shouldn't; even though Mrs. Jordan, handed down from their early twilight of gentility and also the victim of reverses, was the only member of her circle in whom she recognised an equal. She was perfectly aware that her imaginative life was the life in which she spent most of her time; and she would have been ready, had it been at all worth while, to contend that, since her outward occupation didn't kill it, it must be strong indeed.

Combinations of flowers and green-stuff, forsooth! What she could handle freely, she said to herself, was combinations of men and women. The only weakness in her faculty came from the positive abundance of her contact with the human herd; this was so constant, it had so the effect of cheapening her privilege, that there were long stretches in which inspiration, divination and interest quite dropped. The great thing was the flashes, the quick revivals, absolute accidents all, and neither to be counted on nor to be resisted. Some one had only sometimes to put in a penny for a stamp and the whole thing was upon her. She was so absurdly constructed that these were literally the moments that made up—made up for the long stiffness of sitting there in the stocks, made up for the cunning hostility of Mr. Buckton and the importunate sympathy of the counter-clerk, made up for the daily deadly flourishy letter from Mr. Mudge, made up even for the most haunting of her worries, the rage at moments of not knowing how her mother did "get it."

She had surrendered herself moreover of late to a certain expansion of her consciousness; something that seemed perhaps vulgarly accounted for by the fact that, as the blast of the season roared louder and the waves of fashion tossed their spray further over the counter, there were more impressions to be gathered and really—for it came to that—more life to be led. Definite at any rate it was that by the time May was well started the kind of company she kept at Cocker's had begun to strike her as a reason—a reason she might almost put forward for a policy of procrastination. It sounded silly, of course, as yet, to plead such a motive, especially as the fascination of the place was after all a sort of torment. But she liked her torment; it was a torment she should miss at Chalk Farm. She was ingenious and uncandid, therefore, about leaving the breadth of London a little longer between herself and that austerity. If she hadn't quite the courage in short to say to Mr. Mudge that her actual chance for a play of mind was worth any week the three shillings he desired to help her to save, she yet saw something happen in the course of the month that in her heart of hearts at least answered the subtle question. This was connected precisely with the appearance of the memorable lady.

CHAPTER III

She pushed in three bescribbled forms which the girl's hand was quick to appropriate, Mr. Buckton having so frequent a perverse instinct for catching first any eye that promised the sort of entertainment with which she had her peculiar affinity. The amusements of captives are full of a desperate contrivance, and one of our young friend's ha'pennyworths had been the charming tale of "Picciola." It was of course the law of the place that they were never to take no notice, as Mr. Buckton said, whom they served; but this also never prevented, certainly on the same gentleman's own part, what he was fond of describing as the underhand game. Both her companions, for that matter, made no secret of the number of favourites they had among the ladies; sweet familiarities in spite of which she had repeatedly caught each of them in stupidities and mistakes, confusions of identity and lapses of observation that never failed to remind her how the cleverness of men ends where the cleverness of women begins. "Marguerite, Regent Street. Try on at six. All Spanish lace. Pearls. The full length." That was the first; it had no signature. "Lady Agnes Orme, Hyde Park Place. Impossible to-night, dining Haddon. Opera to-morrow, promised Fritz, but could do play Wednesday. Will try Haddon for Savoy, and anything in the world you like, if you can get Gussy. Sunday Montenero. Sit Mason Monday, Tuesday. Marguerite awful. Cissy." That was the second. The third, the girl noted when she took it, was on a foreign form: "Everard, Hôtel Brighton, Paris. Only understand and believe. 22nd to 26th, and certainly 8th and 9th. Perhaps others. Come. Mary."

Mary was very handsome, the handsomest woman, she felt in a moment, she had ever seen—or perhaps it was only Cissy. Perhaps it was both, for she had seen stranger things than that—ladies wiring to different persons under different names. She had seen all sorts of things and pieced together all sorts of mysteries. There had once been one—not long before—who, without winking, sent off five over five different signatures. Perhaps these represented five different friends who had asked her—all women, just as perhaps now Mary and Cissy, or one or other of them, were wiring by deputy. Sometimes she put in too much—too much of her own sense; sometimes she put in too little; and in either case this often came round to her afterwards, for she had an extraordinary way of keeping clues. When she noticed she noticed; that was what it came to. There were days and days, there were weeks sometimes, of vacancy. This arose often from Mr. Buckton's devilish and successful subterfuges for keeping her at the sounder whenever it looked as if anything might arouse; the sounder, which it was equally his business to mind, being the innermost cell of captivity, a cage within the cage, fenced off from the rest by a frame of ground glass. The counter-clerk would have played into her hands; but the counter-clerk was really reduced to idiocy by the effect of his passion for her. She flattered herself moreover, nobly, that with the unpleasant conspicuity of this passion she would never have consented to be obliged to him. The most she would ever do would be always to shove off on him whenever she could the registration of letters, a job she happened particularly to loathe. After the long stupors, at all events, there almost always suddenly would come a sharp taste of something; it was in her mouth before she knew it; it was in her mouth now.

To Cissy, to Mary, whichever it was, she found her curiosity going out with a rush, a mute effusion that floated back to her, like a returning tide, the living colour and splendour of the beautiful head, the light of eyes that seemed to reflect such utterly other things than the mean things actually before them; and, above all, the high curt consideration of a manner that even at bad moments was a magnificent habit and of the very essence of the innumerable things—her beauty, her birth, her father and mother, her cousins and all her ancestors—that its possessor couldn't have got rid of even had she wished. How did our obscure little public servant know that for the lady of the telegrams this was a bad moment? How did she guess all sorts of impossible things, such as, almost on the very spot, the presence of drama at a critical stage and the nature of the tie with the gentleman at the Hôtel Brighton? More than ever before it floated to her through the bars of the cage that this at last was the high reality, the bristling truth that she had hitherto only patched up and eked out—one of the creatures, in fine, in whom all the conditions for happiness actually met, and who, in the air they made, bloomed with an unwitting insolence. What came home to the girl was the way the insolence was tempered by something that was equally a part of the distinguished life, the custom of a flowerlike bend to the less fortunate—a dropped fragrance, a mere quick breath, but which in fact pervaded and lingered. The apparition was very young, but certainly married, and our fatigued friend had a sufficient store of mythological comparison to recognise the port of Juno. Marguerite might be "awful," but she knew how to dress a goddess.

Pearls and Spanish lace—she herself, with assurance, could see them, and the "full length" too, and also red velvet bows, which, disposed on the lace in a particular manner (she could have placed them with the turn of a hand) were of course to adorn the front of a black brocade that would be like a dress in a picture. However, neither Marguerite nor Lady Agnes nor Haddon nor Fritz nor Gussy was what the wearer of this garment had really come in for. She had come in for Everard—and that was doubtless not his true name either. If our young lady had never taken such jumps before it was simply that she had never before been so affected. She went all the way. Mary and Cissy had been round together, in their single superb person, to see him—he must live round the corner; they had found that, in consequence of something they had come, precisely, to make up for or to have another scene about, he had gone off—gone off just on purpose to make them feel it; on which they had come together to Cocker's as to the nearest place; where they had put in the three forms partly in order not to put in the one alone. The two others in a manner, covered it, muffled it, passed it off. Oh yes, she went all the way, and this was a specimen of how she often went. She would know the hand again any time. It was as handsome and as everything else as the woman herself. The woman herself had, on learning his flight, pushed past Everard's servant and into his room; she had written her missive at his table and with his pen. All this, every inch of it, came in the waft that she blew through and left behind her, the influence that, as I have said, lingered. And among the things the girl was sure of, happily, was that she should see her again.

CHAPTER IV

She saw her in fact, and only ten days later; but this time not alone, and that was exactly a part of the luck of it. Not unaware—as how could her observation have left her so?—of the possibilities through which it could range, our young lady had ever since had in her mind a dozen conflicting theories about Everard's type; as to which, the instant they came into the place, she felt the point settled with a thump that seemed somehow addressed straight to her heart. That organ literally beat faster at the approach of the gentleman who was this time with Cissy, and who, as seen from within the cage, became on the spot the happiest of the happy circumstances with which her mind had invested the friend of Fritz and Gussy. He was a very happy circumstance indeed as, with his cigarette in his lips and his broken familiar talk caught by his companion, he put down the half-dozen telegrams it would take them together several minutes to dispatch. And here it occurred, oddly enough, that if, shortly before the girl's interest in his companion had sharpened her sense for the messages then transmitted, her immediate vision of himself had the effect, while she counted his seventy words, of preventing intelligibility. His words were mere numbers, they told her nothing whatever; and after he had gone she was in possession of no name, of no address, of no meaning, of nothing but a vague sweet sound and an immense impression. He had been there but five minutes, he had smoked in her face, and, busy with his telegrams, with the tapping pencil and the conscious danger, the odious betrayal that would come from a mistake, she had had no wandering glances nor roundabout arts to spare. Yet she had taken him in; she knew everything; she had made up her mind.

He had come back from Paris; everything was rearranged; the pair were again shoulder to shoulder in their high encounter with life, their large and complicated game. The fine soundless pulse of this game was in the air for our young woman while they remained in the shop. While they remained? They remained all day; their presence continued and abode with her, was in everything she did till nightfall, in the thousands of other words she counted, she transmitted, in all the stamps she detached and the letters she weighed and the change she gave, equally unconscious and unerring in each of these particulars, and not, as the run on the little office thickened with the afternoon hours, looking up at a single ugly face in the long sequence, nor really hearing the stupid questions that she patiently and perfectly answered. All patience was possible now, all questions were stupid after his, all faces were ugly. She had been sure she should see the lady again; and even now she should perhaps, she should probably, see her often. But for him it was totally different; she should never never see him. She wanted it too much. There was a kind of wanting that helped—she had arrived, with her rich experience, at that generalisation; and there was another kind that was fatal. It was this time the fatal kind; it would prevent.

Well, she saw him the very next day, and on this second occasion it was quite different; the sense of every syllable he paid for was fiercely distinct; she indeed felt her progressive pencil, dabbing as if with a quick caress the marks of his own, put life into every stroke. He was there a long time—had not brought his forms filled out but worked them off in a nook on the counter; and there were other people as well—a changing pushing cluster, with every one to mind at once and endless right change to make and information to produce. But she kept hold of him throughout; she continued, for herself, in a relation with him as close as that in which, behind the hated ground glass, Mr. Buckton luckily continued with the sounder. This morning everything changed, but rather to dreariness; she had to swallow the rebuff to her theory about fatal desires, which she did without confusion and indeed with absolute levity; yet if it was now flagrant that he did live close at hand—at Park Chambers—and belonged supremely to the class that wired everything, even their expensive feelings (so that, as he never wrote, his correspondence cost him weekly pounds and pounds, and he might be in and out five times a day) there was, all the same, involved in the prospect, and by reason of its positive excess of light, a perverse melancholy, a gratuitous misery. This was at once to give it a place in an order of feelings on which I shall presently touch.

Meanwhile, for a month, he was very constant. Cissy, Mary, never re-appeared with him; he was always either alone or accompanied only by some gentleman who was lost in the blaze of his glory. There was another sense, however—and indeed there was more than one—in which she mostly found herself counting in the splendid creature with whom she had originally connected him. He addressed this correspondent neither as Mary nor as Cissy; but the girl was sure of whom it was, in Eaten Square, that he was perpetually wiring to—and all so irreproachably!—as Lady Bradeen. Lady Bradeen was Cissy, Lady Bradeen was Mary, Lady Bradeen was the friend of Fritz and of Gussy, the customer of Marguerite, and the close ally in short (as was ideally right, only the girl had not yet found a descriptive term that was) of the most magnificent of men. Nothing could equal the frequency and variety of his communications to her ladyship but their extraordinary, their abysmal propriety. It was just the talk—so profuse sometimes that she wondered what was left for their real meetings—of the very happiest people. Their real meetings must have been constant, for half of it was appointments and allusions, all swimming in a sea of other allusions still, tangled in a complexity of questions that gave a wondrous image of their life. If Lady Bradeen was Juno it was all certainly Olympian. If the girl, missing the answers, her ladyship's own outpourings, vainly reflected that Cocker's should have been one of the bigger offices where telegrams arrived as well as departed, there were yet ways in which, on the whole, she pressed the romance closer by reason of the very quantity of imagination it demanded and consumed. The days and hours of this new friend, as she came to account him, were at all events unrolled, and however much more she might have known she would still have wished to go beyond. In fact she did go beyond; she went quite far enough.

But she could none the less, even after a month, scarce have told if the gentlemen who came in with him recurred or changed; and this in spite of the fact that they too were always posting and wiring, smoking in her face and signing or not signing. The gentlemen who came in with him were nothing when he was there. They turned up alone at other times—then only perhaps with a dim richness of reference. He himself, absent as well as present, was all. He was very tall, very fair, and had, in spite of his thick preoccupations, a good-humour that was exquisite, particularly as it so often had the effect of keeping him on. He could have reached over anybody, and anybody—no matter who—would have let him; but he was so extraordinarily kind that he quite pathetically waited, never waggling things at her out of his turn nor saying "Here!" with horrid sharpness. He waited for pottering old ladies, for gaping slaveys, for the perpetual Buttonses from Thrupp's; and the thing in all this that she would have liked most unspeakably to put to the test was the possibility of her having for him a personal identity that might in a particular way appeal. There were moments when he actually struck her as on her side, as arranging to help, to support, to spare her.

But such was the singular spirit of our young friend that she could remind herself with a pang that when people had awfully good manners—people of that class,—you couldn't tell. These manners were for everybody, and it might be drearily unavailing for any poor particular body to be overworked and unusual. What he did take for granted was all sorts of facility; and his high pleasantness, his relighting of cigarettes while he waited, his unconscious bestowal of opportunities, of boons, of blessings, were all a part of his splendid security, the instinct that told him there was nothing such an existence as his could ever lose by. He was somehow all at once very bright and very grave, very young and immensely complete; and whatever he was at any moment it was always as much as all the rest the mere bloom of his beatitude. He was sometimes Everard, as he had been at the Hôtel Brighton, and he was sometimes Captain Everard. He was sometimes Philip with his surname and sometimes Philip without it. In some directions he was merely Phil, in others he was merely Captain. There were relations in which he was none of these things, but a quite different person—"the Count." There were several friends for whom he was William. There were several for whom, in allusion perhaps to his complexion, he was "the Pink 'Un." Once, once only by good luck, he had, coinciding comically, quite miraculously, with another person also near to her, been "Mudge." Yes, whatever he was, it was a part of his happiness—whatever he was and probably whatever he wasn't. And his happiness was a part—it became so little by little—of something that, almost from the first of her being at Cocker's, had been deeply with the girl.

CHAPTER V

This was neither more nor less than the queer extension of her experience, the double life that, in the cage, she grew at last to lead. As the weeks went on there she lived more and more into the world of whiffs and glimpses, she found her divinations work faster and stretch further. It was a prodigious view as the pressure heightened, a panorama fed with facts and figures, flushed with a torrent of colour and accompanied with wondrous world-music. What it mainly came to at this period was a picture of how London could amuse itself; and that, with the running commentary of a witness so exclusively a witness, turned for the most part to a hardening of the heart. The nose of this observer was brushed by the bouquet, yet she could never really pluck even a daisy. What could still remain fresh in her daily grind was the immense disparity, the difference and contrast, from class to class, of every instant and every motion. There were times when all the wires in the country seemed to start from the little hole-and-corner where she plied for a livelihood, and where, in the shuffle of feet, the flutter of "forms," the straying of stamps and the ring of change over the counter, the people she had fallen into the habit of remembering and fitting together with others, and of having her theories and interpretations of, kept up before her their long procession and rotation. What twisted the knife in her vitals was the way the profligate rich scattered about them, in extravagant chatter over their extravagant pleasures and sins, an amount of money that would have held the stricken household of her frightened childhood, her poor pinched mother and tormented father and lost brother and starved sister, together for a lifetime. During her first weeks she had often gasped at the sums people were willing to pay for the stuff they transmitted—the "much love"s, the "awful" regrets, the compliments and wonderments and vain vague gestures that cost the price of a new pair of boots. She had had a way then of glancing at the people's faces, but she had early learnt that if you became a telegraphist you soon ceased to be astonished. Her eye for types amounted nevertheless to genius, and there were those she liked and those she hated, her feeling for the latter of which grew to a positive possession, an instinct of observation and detection. There were the brazen women, as she called them, of the higher and the lower fashion, whose squanderings and graspings, whose struggles and secrets and love-affairs and lies, she tracked and stored up against them till she had at moments, in private, a triumphant vicious feeling of mastery and ease, a sense of carrying their silly guilty secrets in her pocket, her small retentive brain, and thereby knowing so much more about them than they suspected or would care to think. There were those she would have liked to betray, to trip up, to bring down with words altered and fatal; and all through a personal hostility provoked by the lightest signs, by their accidents of tone and manner, by the particular kind of relation she always happened instantly to feel.

There were impulses of various kinds, alternately soft and severe, to which she was constitutionally accessible and which were determined by the smallest accidents. She was rigid in general on the article of making the public itself affix its stamps, and found a special enjoyment in dealing to that end with some of the ladies who were too grand to touch them. She had thus a play of refinement and subtlety greater, she flattered herself, than any of which she could be made the subject; and though most people were too stupid to be conscious of this it brought her endless small consolations and revenges. She recognised quite as much those of her sex whom she would have liked to help, to warn, to rescue, to see more of; and that alternative as well operated exactly through the hazard of personal sympathy, her vision for silver threads and moonbeams and her gift for keeping the clues and finding her way in the tangle. The moonbeams and silver threads presented at moments all the vision of what poor she might have made of happiness. Blurred and blank as the whole thing often inevitably, or mercifully, became, she could still, through crevices and crannies, be stupefied, especially by what, in spite of all seasoning, touched the sorest place in her consciousness, the revelation of the golden shower flying about without a gleam of gold for herself. It remained prodigious to the end, the money her fine friends were able to spend to get still more, or even to complain to fine friends of their own that they were in want. The pleasures they proposed were equalled only by those they declined, and they made their appointments often so expensively that she was left wondering at the nature of the delights to which the mere approaches were so paved with shillings. She quivered on occasion into the perception of this and that one whom she would on the chance have just simply liked to be. Her conceit, her baffled vanity, was possibly monstrous; she certainly often threw herself into a defiant conviction that she would have done the whole thing much better. But her greatest comfort, mostly, was her comparative vision of the men; by whom I mean the unmistakeable gentlemen, for she had no interest in the spurious or the shabby and no mercy at all for the poor. She could have found a sixpence, outside, for an appearance of want; but her fancy, in some directions so alert, had never a throb of response for any sign of the sordid. The men she did track, moreover, she tracked mainly in one relation, the relation as to which the cage convinced her, she believed, more than anything else could have done, that it was quite the most diffused.

She found her ladies, in short, almost always in communication with her gentlemen, and her gentlemen with her ladies, and she read into the immensity of their intercourse stories and meanings without end. Incontestably she grew to think that the men cut the best figure; and in this particular, as in many others, she arrived at a philosophy of her own, all made up of her private notations and cynicisms. It was a striking part of the business, for example, that it was much more the women, on the whole, who were after the men than the men who were after the women: it was literally visible that the general attitude of the one sex was that of the object pursued and defensive, apologetic and attenuating, while the light of her own nature helped her more or less to conclude as to the attitude of the other. Perhaps she herself a little even fell into the custom of pursuit in occasionally deviating only for gentlemen from her high rigour about the stamps. She had early in the day made up her mind, in fine, that they had the best manners; and if there were none of them she noticed when Captain Everard was there, there were plenty she could place and trace and name at other times, plenty who, with their way of being "nice" to her, and of handling, as if their pockets were private tills loose mixed masses of silver and gold, were such pleasant appearances that she could envy them without dislike. They never had to give change—they only had to get it. They ranged through every suggestion, every shade of fortune, which evidently included indeed lots of bad luck as well as of good, declining even toward Mr. Mudge and his bland firm thrift, and ascending, in wild signals and rocket-flights, almost to within hail of her highest standard. So from month to month she went on with them all, through a thousand ups and downs and a thousand pangs and indifferences. What virtually happened was that in the shuffling herd that passed before her by far the greater part only passed—a proportion but just appreciable stayed. Most of the elements swam straight away, lost themselves in the bottomless common, and by so doing really kept the page clear. On the clearness therefore what she did retain stood sharply out; she nipped and caught it, turned it over and interwove it.

CHAPTER VI

She met Mrs. Jordan when she could, and learned from her more and more how the great people, under her gentle shake and after going through everything with the mere shops, were waking up to the gain of putting into the hands of a person of real refinement the question that the shop-people spoke of so vulgarly as that of the floral decorations. The regular dealers in these decorations were all very well; but there was a peculiar magic in the play of taste of a lady who had only to remember, through whatever intervening dusk, all her own little tables, little bowls and little jars and little other arrangements, and the wonderful thing she had made of the garden of the vicarage. This small domain, which her young friend had never seen, bloomed in Mrs. Jordan's discourse like a new Eden, and she converted the past into a bank of violets by the tone in which she said "Of course you always knew my one passion!" She obviously met now, at any rate, a big contemporary need, measured what it was rapidly becoming for people to feel they could trust her without a tremor. It brought them a peace that—during the quarter of an hour before dinner in especial—was worth more to them than mere payment could express. Mere payment, none the less, was tolerably prompt; she engaged by the month, taking over the whole thing; and there was an evening on which, in respect to our heroine, she at last returned to the charge. "It's growing and growing, and I see that I must really divide the work. One wants an associate—of one's own kind, don't you know? You know the look they want it all to have?—of having come, not from a florist, but from one of themselves. Well, I'm sure you could give it—because you are one. Then we should win. Therefore just come in with me."

"And leave the P.O.?"

"Let the P.O. simply bring you your letters. It would bring you lots, you'd see: orders, after a bit, by the score." It was on this, in due course, that the great advantage again came up: "One seems to live again with one's own people." It had taken some little time (after their having parted company in the tempest of their troubles and then, in the glimmering dawn, finally sighted each other again) for each to admit that the other was, in her private circle, her only equal, but the admission came, when it did come, with an honest groan; and since equality was named, each found much personal profit in exaggerating the other's original grandeur. Mrs. Jordan was ten years the older, but her young friend was struck with the smaller difference this now made: it had counted otherwise at the time when, much more as a friend of her mother's, the bereaved lady, without a penny of provision and with stopgaps, like their own, all gone, had, across the sordid landing on which the opposite doors of the pair of scared miseries opened and to which they were bewilderedly bolted, borrowed coals and umbrellas that were repaid in potatoes and postage-stamps. It had been a questionable help, at that time, to ladies submerged, floundering, panting, swimming for their lives, that they were ladies; but such an advantage could come up again in proportion as others vanished, and it had grown very great by the time it was the only ghost of one they possessed. They had literally watched it take to itself a portion of the substance of each that had departed; and it became prodigious now, when they could talk of it together, when they could look back at it across a desert of accepted derogation, and when, above all, they could together work up a credulity about it that neither could otherwise work up. Nothing was really so marked as that they felt the need to cultivate this legend much more after having found their feet and stayed their stomachs in the ultimate obscure than they had done in the upper air of mere frequent shocks. The thing they could now oftenest say to each other was that they knew what they meant; and the sentiment with which, all round, they knew it was known had well-nigh amounted to a promise not again to fall apart.

Mrs. Jordan was at present fairly dazzling on the subject of the way that, in the practice of her fairy art, as she called it, she more than peeped in—she penetrated. There was not a house of the great kind—and it was of course only a question of those, real homes of luxury—in which she was not, at the rate such people now had things, all over the place. The girl felt before the picture the cold breath of disinheritance as much as she had ever felt it in the cage; she knew moreover how much she betrayed this, for the experience of poverty had begun, in her life, too early, and her ignorance of the requirements of homes of luxury had grown, with other active knowledge, a depth of simplification. She had accordingly at first often found that in these colloquies she could only pretend she understood. Educated as she had rapidly been by her chances at Cocker's, there were still strange gaps in her learning—she could never, like Mrs. Jordan, have found her way about one of the "homes." Little by little, however, she had caught on, above all in the light of what Mrs. Jordan's redemption had materially made of that lady, giving her, though the years and the struggles had naturally not straightened a feature, an almost super-eminent air. There were women in and out of

Cocker's who were quite nice and who yet didn't look well; whereas Mrs. Jordan looked well and yet, with her extraordinarily protrusive teeth, was by no means quite nice. It would seem, mystifyingly, that it might really come from all the greatness she could live with. It was fine to hear her talk so often of dinners of twenty and of her doing, as she said, exactly as she liked with them. She spoke as if, for that matter, she invited the company. "They simply give me the table—all the rest, all the other effects, come afterwards."

CHAPTER VII

"Then you do see them?" the girl again asked.

Mrs. Jordan hesitated, and indeed the point had been ambiguous before. "Do you mean the guests?"

Her young friend, cautious about an undue exposure of innocence, was not quite sure. "Well—the people who live there."

"Lady Ventnor? Mrs. Bubb? Lord Rye? Dear, yes. Why they like one."

"But does one personally know them?" our young lady went on, since that was the way to speak. "I mean socially, don't you know?—as you know me."

"They're not so nice as you!" Mrs. Jordan charmingly cried. "But I shall see more and more of them."

Ah this was the old story. "But how soon?"

"Why almost any day. Of course," Mrs. Jordan honestly added, "they're nearly always out."

"Then why do they want flowers all over?"

"Oh that doesn't make any difference." Mrs. Jordan was not philosophic; she was just evidently determined it shouldn't make any. "They're awfully interested in my ideas, and it's inevitable they should meet me over them."

Her interlocutress was sturdy enough. "What do you call your ideas?"

Mrs. Jordan's reply was fine. "If you were to see me some day with a thousand tulips you'd discover."

"A thousand?"—the girl gaped at such a revelation of the scale of it; she felt for the instant fairly planted out. "Well, but if in fact they never do meet you?" she none the less pessimistically insisted.

"Never? They often do—and evidently quite on purpose. We have grand long talks."

There was something in our young lady that could still stay her from asking for a personal description of these apparitions; that showed too starved a state. But while she considered she took in afresh the whole of the clergyman's widow. Mrs. Jordan couldn't help her teeth, and her sleeves were a distinct rise in the world. A thousand tulips at a shilling clearly took one further than a thousand words at a penny; and the betrothed of Mr. Mudge, in whom the sense of the race for life was always acute, found herself wondering, with a twinge of her easy jealousy, if it mightn't after all then, for her also, be better—better than where she was—to follow some such scent. Where she was was where Mr. Buckton's elbow could freely enter her right side and the counter-clerk's breathing—he had something the matter with his nose—pervade her left ear. It was something to fill an office under Government, and she knew but too well there were places commoner still than Cocker's; but it needed no great range of taste to bring home to her the picture of servitude and promiscuity she couldn't but offer to the eye of comparative freedom. She was so boxed up with her young men, and anything like a margin so absent, that it needed more art than she should ever possess to pretend in the least to compass, with any one in the nature of an acquaintance—say with Mrs. Jordan herself, flying in, as it might happen, to wire sympathetically to Mrs. Bubb—an approach to a relation of elegant privacy. She remembered the day when Mrs. Jordan had, in fact, by the greatest chance, come in with fifty-three words for Lord Rye and a five-pound note to change. This had been the dramatic manner of their reunion—their mutual recognition was so great an event. The girl could at first only see her from the waist up, besides making but little of her long telegram to his lordship. It was a strange whirligig that had converted the clergyman's widow into such a specimen of the class that went beyond the sixpence.

Nothing of the occasion, all the more, had ever become dim; least of all the way that, as her recovered friend looked up from counting, Mrs. Jordan had just blown, in explanation, through her teeth and through the bars of the cage: "I do flowers, you know." Our young woman had always, with her little finger crooked out, a pretty movement for counting; and she had not forgotten the small secret advantage, a sharpness of triumph it might even have been called, that fell upon her at this moment and avenged her for the incoherence of the message, an unintelligible enumeration of numbers, colours, days, hours. The correspondence of people she didn't know was one thing; but the correspondence of people she did had an aspect of its own for her even when she couldn't understand it. The speech in which Mrs. Jordan had defined a position and announced a profession was like a tinkle of bluebells; but for herself her one idea about flowers was that people had them at funerals, and her present sole gleam of light was that lords probably had them most. When she watched, a minute later, through the cage, the swing of her visitor's departing petticoats, she saw the sight from the waist down; and when the counter-clerk, after a mere male glance, remarked, with an intention unmistakeably low, "Handsome woman!" she had for him the finest of her chills: "She's the widow of a bishop." She always felt, with the counter-clerk, that it was impossible sufficiently to put it on; for what she wished to express to him was the maximum of her contempt, and that element in her nature was confusedly stored. "A bishop" was putting it on, but the counter-clerk's approaches were vile. The night, after this, when, in the fulness of time, Mrs. Jordan mentioned the grand long talks, the girl at last brought out: "Should I see them?—I mean if I were to give up everything for you."

Mrs. Jordan at this became most arch. "I'd send you to all the bachelors!"

Our young lady could be reminded by such a remark that she usually struck her friend as pretty. "Do they have their flowers?"

"Oceans. And they're the most particular." Oh it was a wonderful world. "You should see Lord Rye's."

"His flowers?"

"Yes, and his letters. He writes me pages on pages—with the most adorable little drawings and plans. You should see his diagrams!"

CHAPTER VIII

The girl had in course of time every opportunity to inspect these documents, and they a little disappointed her; but in the mean while there had been more talk, and it had led to her saying, as if her friend's guarantee of a life of elegance were not quite definite: "Well, I see every one at my place."

"Every one?"

"Lots of swells. They flock. They live, you know, all round, and the place is filled with all the smart people, all the fast people, those whose names are in the papers—mamma has still The Morning Post—and who come up for the season."

Mrs. Jordan took this in with complete intelligence. "Yes, and I dare say it's some of your people that I do."

Her companion assented, but discriminated. "I doubt if you 'do' them as much as I! Their affairs, their appointments and arrangements, their little games and secrets and vices—those things all pass before me."

This was a picture that could make a clergyman's widow not imperceptibly gasp; it was in intention moreover something of a retort to the thousand tulips. "Their vices? Have they got vices?"

Our young critic even more overtly stared then with a touch of contempt in her amusement: "Haven't you found that out?" The homes of luxury then hadn't so much to give. "I find out everything."

Mrs. Jordan, at bottom a very meek person, was visibly struck. "I see. You do 'have' them."

"Oh I don't care! Much good it does me!"

Mrs. Jordan after an instant recovered her superiority. "No—it doesn't lead to much." Her own initiations so clearly did. Still—after all; and she was not jealous: "There must be a charm."

"In seeing them?" At this the girl suddenly let herself go. "I hate them. There's that charm!"

Mrs. Jordan gaped again. "The real 'smarts'?"

"Is that what you call Mrs. Bubb? Yes—it comes to me; I've had Mrs. Bubb. I don't think she has been in herself, but there are things her maid has brought. Well, my dear!"—and the young person from Cocker's, recalling these things and summing them up, seemed suddenly to have much to say. She didn't say it, however; she checked it; she only brought out: "Her maid, who's horrid—she must have her!" Then she went on with indifference: "They're too real! They're selfish brutes."

Mrs. Jordan, turning it over, adopted at last the plan of treating it with a smile. She wished to be liberal. "Well, of course, they do lay it out."

"They bore me to death," her companion pursued with slightly more temperance.

But this was going too far. "Ah that's because you've no sympathy!"

The girl gave an ironic laugh, only retorting that nobody could have any who had to count all day all the words in the dictionary; a contention Mrs. Jordan quite granted, the more that she shuddered at the notion of ever failing of the very gift to which she owed the vogue—the rage she might call it—that had caught her up. Without sympathy—or without imagination, for it came back again to that—how should she get, for big dinners, down the middle and toward the far corners at all? It wasn't the combinations, which were easily managed: the strain was over the ineffable simplicities, those that the bachelors above all, and Lord Rye perhaps most of any, threw off—just blew off like cigarette-puffs—such sketches of. The betrothed of Mr. Mudge at all events accepted the explanation, which had the effect, as almost any turn of their talk was now apt to have, of bringing her round to the terrific question of that gentleman. She was tormented with the desire to get out of Mrs. Jordan, on this subject, what she was sure was at the back of Mrs. Jordan's head; and to get it out of her, queerly enough, if only to vent a certain irritation at it. She knew that what her friend would already have risked if she hadn't been timid and tortuous was: "Give him up—yes, give him up: you'll see that with your sure chances you'll be able to do much better."

Our young woman had a sense that if that view could only be put before her with a particular sniff for poor Mr. Mudge she should hate it as much as she morally ought. She was conscious of not, as yet, hating it quite so much as that. But she saw that Mrs. Jordan was conscious of something too, and that there was a degree of confidence she was waiting little by little to arrive at. The day came when the girl caught a glimpse of what was still wanting to make her friend feel strong; which was nothing less than the prospect of being able to announce the climax of sundry private dreams. The associate of the aristocracy had personal calculations—matter for brooding and dreaming, even for peeping out not quite hopelessly from behind the window-curtains of lonely lodgings. If she did the flowers for the bachelors, in short, didn't she expect that to have consequences very different from such an outlook at Cocker's as she had pronounced wholly desperate? There seemed in very truth something auspicious in the mixture of bachelors and flowers, though, when looked hard in the eye, Mrs. Jordan was not quite prepared to say she had expected a positive proposal from Lord Rye to pop out of it. Our young woman arrived at last, none the less, at a definite vision of what was in her mind. This was a vivid foreknowledge that the betrothed of Mr. Mudge would, unless conciliated in advance by a successful rescue, almost hate her on the day she should break a particular piece of news. How could that unfortunate otherwise endure to hear of what, under the protection of Lady Ventnor, was after all so possible.

CHAPTER IX

Meanwhile, since irritation sometimes relieved her, the betrothed of Mr. Mudge found herself indebted to that admirer for amounts of it perfectly proportioned to her fidelity. She always walked with him on Sundays, usually in the Regent's Park, and quite often, once or twice a month he took her, in the Strand or thereabouts, to see a piece that was having a run. The productions he always preferred were the really good ones—Shakespeare, Thompson or some funny American thing; which, as it also happened that she hated vulgar plays, gave him ground for what was almost the fondest of his approaches, the theory that their tastes were, blissfully, just the same. He was for ever reminding her of that, rejoicing over it and being affectionate and wise about it. There were times when she wondered how in the world she could "put up with" him, how she could put up with any man so smugly unconscious of the immensity of her difference. It was just for this difference that, if she was to be liked at all, she wanted to be liked, and if that was not the source of Mr. Mudge's admiration, she asked herself what on earth could be? She was not different only at one point, she was different all round; unless perhaps indeed in being practically human, which her mind just barely recognised that he also was. She would have made tremendous concessions in other quarters: there was no limit for instance to those she would have made to Captain Everard; but what I have named was the most she was prepared to do for Mr. Mudge. It was because he was different that, in the oddest way, she liked as well as deplored him; which was after all a proof that the disparity, should they frankly recognise it, wouldn't necessarily be fatal. She felt that, oleaginous—too oleaginous—as he was, he was somehow comparatively primitive: she had once, during the portion of his time at Cocker's that had overlapped her own, seen him collar a drunken soldier, a big violent man who, having come in with a mate to get a postal-order cashed, had made a grab at the money before his friend could reach it and had so determined, among the hams and cheeses and the lodgers from Thrupp's, immediate and alarming reprisals, a scene of scandal and consternation. Mr. Buckton and the counter-clerk had crouched within the cage, but Mr. Mudge had, with a very quiet but very quick step round the counter, an air of masterful authority she shouldn't soon forget, triumphantly interposed in the scrimmage, parted the combatants and shaken the delinquent in his skin. She had been proud of him at that moment, and had felt that if their affair had not already been settled the neatness of his execution would have left her without resistance.

Their affair had been settled by other things: by the evident sincerity of his passion and by the sense that his high white apron resembled a front of many floors. It had gone a great way with her that he would build up a business to his chin, which he carried quite in the air. This could only be a question of time; he would have all Piccadilly in the pen behind his ear. That was a merit in itself for a girl who had known what she had known. There were hours at which she even found him good-looking, though, frankly there could be no crown for her effort to imagine on the part of the tailor or the barber some such treatment of his appearance as would make him resemble even remotely a man of the world. His very beauty was the beauty of a grocer, and the finest future would offer it none too much room consistently to develop. She had engaged herself in short to the perfection of a type, and almost anything square and smooth and whole had its weight for a person still conscious herself of being a mere bruised fragment of wreckage. But it contributed hugely at present to carry on the two parallel lines of her experience in the cage and her experience out of it. After keeping quiet for some time about this opposition she suddenly—one Sunday afternoon on a penny chair in the Regent's Park—broke, for him, capriciously, bewilderingly, into an intimation of what it came to. He had naturally pressed more and more on the point of her again placing herself where he could see her hourly, and for her to recognise that she had as yet given him no sane reason for delay he had small need to describe himself as unable to make out what she was up to. As if, with her absurd bad reasons, she could have begun to tell him! Sometimes she thought it would be amusing to let him have them full in the face, for she felt she should die of him unless she once in a while stupefied him; and sometimes she thought it would be disgusting and perhaps even fatal. She liked him, however, to think her silly, for that gave her the margin which at the best she would always require; and the only difficulty about this was that he hadn't enough imagination to oblige her. It produced none the less something of the desired effect—to leave him simply wondering why, over the matter of their reunion, she didn't yield to his arguments. Then at last, simply as if by accident and out of mere boredom on a day that was rather flat, she preposterously produced her own. "Well, wait a bit. Where I am I still see things." And she talked to him even worse, if possible, than she had talked to Jordan.

Little by little, to her own stupefaction, she caught that he was trying to take it as she meant it and that he was neither astonished nor angry. Oh the British tradesman—this gave her an idea of his resources! Mr. Mudge would be angry only with a person who, like the drunken soldier in the shop, should have an unfavourable effect on business. He seemed positively to enter, for the time and without the faintest flash of irony or ripple of laughter, into the whimsical grounds of her enjoyment of Cocker's custom, and instantly to be casting up whatever it might, as Mrs. Jordan had said, lead to. What he had in mind was not of course what Mrs. Jordan had had: it was obviously not a source of speculation with him that his sweetheart might pick up a husband. She could see perfectly that this was not for a moment even what he supposed she herself dreamed of. What she had done was simply to give his sensibility another push into the dim vast of trade. In that direction it was all alert, and she had whisked before it the mild fragrance of a "connexion." That was the most he could see in any account of her keeping in, on whatever roundabout lines, with the gentry; and when, getting to the bottom of this, she quickly proceeded to show him the kind of eye she turned on such people and to give him a sketch of what that eye discovered, she reduced him to the particular prostration in which he could still be amusing to her.

CHAPTER X

"They're the most awful wretches, I assure you—the lot all about there."

"Then why do you want to stay among them?"

"My dear man, just because they are. It makes me hate them so."

"Hate them? I thought you liked them."

"Don't be stupid. What I 'like' is just to loathe them. You wouldn't believe what passes before my eyes."

"Then why have you never told me? You didn't mention anything before I left."

"Oh I hadn't got round to it then. It's the sort of thing you don't believe at first; you have to look round you a bit and then you understand. You work into it more and more. Besides," the girl went on, "this is the time of the year when the worst lot come up. They're simply packed together in those smart streets. Talk of the numbers of the poor! What I can vouch for is the numbers of the rich! There are new ones every day, and they seem to get richer and richer. Oh, they do come up!" she cried, imitating for her private recreation—she was sure it wouldn't reach Mr. Mudge—the low intonation of the counter-clerk.

"And where do they come from?" her companion candidly enquired.

She had to think a moment; then she found something. "From the 'spring meetings.' They bet tremendously."

"Well, they bet enough at Chalk Farm, if that's all."

"It isn't all. It isn't a millionth part!" she replied with some sharpness. "It's immense fun"—she had to tantalise him. Then as she had heard Mrs. Jordan say, and as the ladies at Cocker's even sometimes wired, "It's quite too dreadful!" She could fully feel how it was Mr. Mudge's propriety, which was extreme—he had a horror of coarseness and attended a Wesleyan chapel—that prevented his asking for details. But she gave him some of the more innocuous in spite of himself, especially putting before him how, at Simpkin's and Ladle's, they all made the money fly. That was indeed what he liked to hear: the connexion was not direct, but one was somehow more in the right place where the money was flying than where it was simply and meagrely nesting. The air felt that stir, he had to acknowledge, much less at Chalk Farm than in the district in which his beloved so oddly enjoyed her footing. She gave him, she could see, a restless sense that these might be familiarities not to be sacrificed; germs, possibilities, faint foreshowings—heaven knew what—of the initiation it would prove profitable to have arrived at when in the fulness of time he should have his own shop in some such paradise. What really touched him—that was discernible—was that she could feed him with so much mere vividness of reminder, keep before him, as by the play of a fan, the very wind of the swift bank-notes and the charm of the existence of a class that Providence had raised up to be the blessing of grocers. He liked to think that the class was there, that it was always there, and that she contributed in her slight but appreciable degree to keep it up to the mark. He couldn't have formulated his theory of the matter, but the exuberance of the aristocracy was the advantage of trade, and everything was knit together in a richness of pattern that it was good to follow with one's finger-tips. It was a comfort to him to be thus assured that there were no symptoms of a drop. What did the sounder, as she called it, nimbly worked, do but keep the ball going?

What it came to therefore for Mr. Mudge was that all enjoyments were, as might be said, inter-related, and that the more people had the more they wanted to have. The more flirtations, as he might roughly express it, the more cheese and pickles. He had even in his own small way been dimly struck with the linkèd sweetness connecting the tender passion with cheap champagne, or perhaps the other way round. What he would have liked to say had he been able to work out his thought to the end was: "I see, I see. Lash them up then, lead them on, keep them going: some of it can't help, some time, coming our way." Yet he was troubled by the suspicion of subtleties on his companion's part that spoiled the straight view. He couldn't understand people's hating what they liked or liking what they hated; above all it hurt him somewhere—for he had his private delicacies—to see anything but money made out of his betters. To be too enquiring, or in any other way too free, at the expense of the gentry was vaguely wrong; the only thing that was distinctly right was to be prosperous at any price. Wasn't it just because they were up there aloft that they were lucrative? He concluded at any rate by saying to his young friend: "If it's improper for you to remain at Cocker's, then that falls in exactly with the other reasons I've put before you for your removal."

"Improper?"—her smile became a prolonged boldness. "My dear boy, there's no one like you!"

"I dare say," he laughed; "but that doesn't help the question."

"Well," she returned, "I can't give up my friends. I'm making even more than Mrs. Jordan."

Mr. Mudge considered. "How much is she making?"

"Oh you dear donkey!"—and, regardless of all the Regent's Park, she patted his cheek. This was the sort of moment at which she was absolutely tempted to tell him that she liked to be near Park Chambers. There was a fascination in the idea of seeing if, on a mention of Captain Everard, he wouldn't do what she thought he might; wouldn't weigh against the obvious objection the still more obvious advantage. The advantage of course could only strike him at the best as rather fantastic; but it was always to the good to keep hold when you had hold, and such an attitude would also after all involve a high tribute to her fidelity. Of one thing she absolutely never doubted: Mr. Mudge believed in her with a belief—! She believed in herself too, for that matter: if there was a thing in the world no one could charge her with it was being the kind of low barmaid person who rinsed tumblers and bandied slang. But she forbore as yet to speak; she had not spoken even to Mrs. Jordan; and the hush that on her lips surrounded the Captain's name maintained itself as a kind of symbol of the success that, up to this time, had attended something or other—she couldn't have said what—that she humoured herself with calling, without words, her relation with him.

CHAPTER XI

She would have admitted indeed that it consisted of little more than the fact that his absences, however frequent and however long, always ended with his turning up again. It was nobody's business in the world but her own if that fact continued to be enough for her. It was of course not enough just in itself; what it had taken on to make it so was the extraordinary possession of the elements of his life that memory and attention had at last given her. There came a day when this possession on the girl's part actually seemed to enjoy between them, while their eyes met, a tacit recognition that was half a joke and half a deep solemnity. He bade her good morning always now; he often quite raised his hat to her. He passed a remark when there was time or room, and once she went so far as to say to him that she hadn't seen him for "ages." "Ages" was the word she consciously and carefully, though a trifle tremulously used; "ages" was exactly what she meant. To this he replied in terms doubtless less anxiously selected, but perhaps on that account not the less remarkable, "Oh yes, hasn't it been awfully wet?" That was a specimen of their give and take; it fed her fancy that no form of intercourse so transcendent and distilled had ever been established on earth. Everything, so far as they chose to consider it so, might mean almost anything. The want of margin in the cage, when he peeped through the bars, wholly ceased to be appreciable. It was a drawback only in superficial commerce. With Captain Everard she had simply the margin of the universe. It may be imagined therefore how their unuttered reference to all she knew about him could in this immensity play at its ease. Every time he handed in a telegram it was an addition to her knowledge: what did his constant smile mean to mark if it didn't mean to mark that? He never came into the place without saying to her in this manner: "Oh yes, you have me by this time so completely at your mercy that it doesn't in the least matter what I give you now. You've become a comfort, I assure you!"

She had only two torments; the greatest of which was that she couldn't, not even once or twice, touch with him on some individual fact. She would have given anything to have been able to allude to one of his friends by name, to one of his engagements by date, to one of his difficulties by the solution. She would have given almost as much for just the right chance—it would have to be tremendously right—to show him in some sharp sweet way that she had perfectly penetrated the greatest of these last and now lived with it in a kind of heroism of sympathy. He was in love with a woman to whom, and to any view of whom, a lady-telegraphist, and especially one who passed a life among hams and cheeses, was as the sand on the floor; and what her dreams desired was the possibility of its somehow coming to him that her own interest in him could take a pure and noble account of such an infatuation and even of such an impropriety. As yet, however, she could only rub along with the hope that an accident, sooner or later, might give her a lift toward popping out with something that would surprise and perhaps even, some fine day, assist him. What could people mean moreover—cheaply sarcastic people—by not feeling all that could be got out of the weather? She felt it all, and seemed literally to feel it most when she went quite wrong, speaking of the stuffy days as cold, of the cold ones as stuffy, and betraying how little she knew, in her cage, of whether it was foul or fair. It was for that matter always stuffy at Cocker's, and she finally settled down to the safe proposition that the outside element was "changeable." Anything seemed true that made him so radiantly assent.

This indeed is a small specimen of her cultivation of insidious ways of making things easy for him—ways to which of course she couldn't be at all sure he did real justice. Real justice was not of this world: she had had too often to come back to that; yet, strangely, happiness was, and her traps had to be set for it in a manner to keep them unperceived by Mr. Buckton and the counter-clerk. The most she could hope for apart from the question, which constantly flickered up and died down, of the divine chance of his consciously liking her, would be that, without analysing it, he should arrive at a vague sense that Cocker's was—well, attractive; easier, smoother, sociably brighter, slightly more picturesque, in short more propitious in general to his little affairs, than any other establishment just thereabouts. She was quite aware that they couldn't be, in so huddled a hole, particularly quick; but she found her account in the slowness—she certainly could bear it if he could. The great pang was that just thereabouts post-offices were so awfully thick. She was always seeing him in imagination in other places and with other girls. But she would defy any other girl to follow him as she followed. And though they weren't, for so many reasons, quick at Cocker's, she could hurry for him when, through an intimation light as air, she gathered that he was pressed.

When hurry was, better still, impossible, it was because of the pleasantest thing of all, the particular element of their contact—she would have called it their friendship—that consisted of an almost humorous treatment of the look of some of his words. They would never perhaps have grown half so intimate if he had not, by the blessing of heaven, formed some of his letters with a queerness—! It was positive that the queerness could scarce have been greater if he had practised it for the very purpose of bringing their heads together over it as far as was possible to heads on different sides of a wire fence. It had taken her truly but once or twice to master these tricks, but, at the cost of striking him perhaps as stupid, she could still challenge them when circumstances favoured. The great circumstance that favoured was that she sometimes actually believed he knew she only feigned perplexity. If he knew it therefore he tolerated it; if he tolerated it he came back; and if he came back he liked her. This was her seventh heaven; and she didn't ask much of his liking—she only asked of it to reach the point of his not going away because of her own. He had at times to be away for weeks; he had to lead lets life; he had to travel—there were places to which he was constantly wiring for "rooms": all this she granted him, forgave him; in fact, in the long run, literally blessed and thanked him for. If he had to lead his life, that precisely fostered his leading it so much by telegraph: therefore the benediction was to come in when he could. That was all she asked—that he shouldn't wholly deprive her.

Sometimes she almost felt that he couldn't have deprived her even had he been minded, by reason of the web of revelation that was woven between them. She quite thrilled herself with thinking what, with such a lot of material, a bad girl would do. It would be a scene better than many in her ha'penny novels, this going to him in the dusk of evening at Park Chambers and letting him at last have it. "I know too much about a certain person now not to put it to you—excuse my being so lurid—that it's quite worth your while to buy me off. Come, therefore; buy me!" There was a point indeed at which such flights had to drop again—the point of an unreadiness to name, when it came to that, the purchasing medium. It wouldn't certainly be anything so gross as money, and the matter accordingly remained rather vague, all the more that she was not a bad girl. It wasn't for any such reason as might have aggravated a mere minx that she often hoped he would again bring Cissy. The difficulty of this, however, was constantly present to her, for the kind of communion to which Cocker's so richly ministered rested on the fact that Cissy and he were so often in different places. She knew by this time all the places—Suchbury, Monkhouse, Whiteroy, Finches—and even how the parties on these occasions were composed; but her subtlety found ways to make her knowledge fairly protect and promote their keeping, as she had heard Mrs. Jordan say, in touch. So, when he actually sometimes smiled as if he really felt the awkwardness of giving her again one of the same old addresses, all her being went out in the desire—which her face must have expressed—that he should recognise her forbearance to criticise as one of the finest tenderest sacrifices a woman had ever made for love.

CHAPTER XII

She was occasionally worried, however this might be, by the impression that these sacrifices, great as they were, were nothing to those that his own passion had imposed; if indeed it was not rather the passion of his confederate, which had caught him up and was whirling him round like a great steam-wheel. He was at any rate in the strong grip of a dizzy splendid fate; the wild wind of his life blew him straight before it. Didn't she catch in his face at times, even through his smile and his happy habit, the gleam of that pale glare with which a bewildered victim appeals, as he passes, to some pair of pitying eyes? He perhaps didn't even himself know how scared he was; but she knew. They were in danger, they were in danger, Captain Everard and Lady Bradeen: it beat every novel in the shop. She thought of Mr. Mudge and his safe sentiment; she thought of herself and blushed even more for her tepid response to it. It was a comfort to her at such moments to feel that in another relation—a relation supplying that affinity with her nature that Mr. Mudge, deluded creature, would never supply—she should have been no more tepid than her ladyship. Her deepest soundings were on two or three occasions of finding herself almost sure that, if she dared, her ladyship's lover would have gathered relief from "speaking" to her. She literally fancied once or twice that, projected as he was toward his doom, her own eyes struck him, while the air roared in his ears, as the one pitying pair in the crowd. But how could he speak to her while she sat sandwiched there between the counter-clerk and the sounder?

She had long ago, in her comings and goings made acquaintance with Park Chambers and reflected as she looked up at their luxurious front that they of course would supply the ideal setting for the ideal speech. There was not an object in London that, before the season was over, was more stamped upon her brain. She went roundabout to pass it, for it was not on the short way; she passed on the opposite side of the street and always looked up, though it had taken her a long time to be sure of the particular set of windows. She had made that out finally by an act of audacity that at the time had almost stopped her heartbeats and that in retrospect greatly quickened her blushes. One evening she had lingered late and watched—watched for some moment when the porter, who was in uniform and often on the steps, had gone in with a visitor. Then she followed boldly, on the calculation that he would have taken the visitor up and that the hall would be free. The hall was free, and the electric light played over the gilded and lettered board that showed the names and numbers of the occupants of the different floors. What she wanted looked straight at her—Captain Everard was on the third. It was as if, in the immense intimacy of this, they were, for the instant and the first time, face to face outside the cage. Alas! they were face to face but a second or two: she was whirled out on the wings of a panic fear that he might just then be entering or issuing. This fear was indeed, in her shameless deflexions, never very far from her, and was mixed in the oddest way with depressions and disappointments. It was dreadful, as she trembled by, to run the risk of looking to him as if she basely hung about; and yet it was dreadful to be obliged to pass only at such moments as put an encounter out of the question.

At the horrible hour of her first coming to Cocker's he was always—it was to be hoped—snug in bed; and at the hour of her final departure he was of course—she had such things all on her fingers'-ends—dressing for dinner. We may let it pass that if she couldn't bring herself to hover till he was dressed, this was simply because such a process for such a person could only be terribly prolonged. When she went in the middle of the day to her own dinner she had too little time to do anything but go straight, though it must be added that for a real certainty she would joyously have omitted the repast. She had made up her mind as to there being on the whole no decent pretext to justify her flitting casually past at three o'clock in the morning. That was the hour at which, if the ha'penny novels were not all wrong, he probably came home for the night. She was therefore reduced to the vainest figuration of the miraculous meeting toward which a hundred impossibilities would have to conspire. But if nothing was more impossible than the fact, nothing was more intense than the vision. What may not, we can only moralise, take place in the quickened muffled perception of a young person with an ardent soul? All our humble friend's native distinction, her refinement of personal grain, of heredity, of pride, took refuge in this small throbbing spot; for when she was most conscious of the objection of her vanity and the pitifulness of her little flutters and manoeuvres, then the consolation and the redemption were most sure to glow before her in some just discernible sign. He did like her!

CHAPTER XIII

He never brought Cissy back, but Cissy came one day without him, as fresh as before from the hands of Marguerite, or only, at the season's end, a trifle less fresh. She was, however, distinctly less serene. She had brought nothing with her and looked about with impatience for the forms and the place to write. The latter convenience, at Cocker's, was obscure and barely adequate, and her clear voice had the light note of disgust which her lover's never showed as she responded with a "There?" of surprise to the gesture made by the counter-clerk in answer to her sharp question. Our young friend was busy with half a dozen people, but she had dispatched them in her most businesslike manner by the time her ladyship flung through the bars this light of re-appearance. Then the directness with which the girl managed to receive the accompanying missive was the result of the concentration that had caused her to make the stamps fly during the few minutes occupied by the production of it. This concentration, in turn, may be described as the effect of the apprehension of imminent relief. It was nineteen days, counted and checked off, since she had seen the object of her homage; and as, had he been in London, she should, with his habits, have been sure to see him often, she was now about to learn what other spot his presence might just then happen to sanctify. For she thought of them, the other spots, as ecstatically conscious of it, expressively happy in it.

But, gracious, how handsome was her ladyship, and what an added price it gave him that the air of intimacy he threw out should have flowed originally from such a source! The girl looked straight through the cage at the eyes and lips that must so often have been so near as own—looked at them with a strange passion that for an instant had the result of filling out some of the gaps, supplying the missing answers, in his correspondence. Then as she made out that the features she thus scanned and associated were totally unaware of it, that they glowed only with the colour of quite other and not at all guessable thoughts, this directly added to their splendour, gave the girl the sharpest impression she had yet received of the uplifted, the unattainable plains of heaven, and yet at the same time caused her to thrill with a sense of the high company she did somehow keep. She was with the absent through her ladyship and with her ladyship through the absent. The only pang—but it didn't matter—was the proof in the admirable face, in the sightless preoccupation of its possessor, that the latter hadn't a notion of her. Her folly had gone to the point of half believing that the other party to the affair must sometimes mention in Eaton Square the extraordinary little person at the place from which he so often wired. Yet the perception of her visitor's blankness actually helped this extraordinary little person, the next instant, to take refuge in a reflexion that could be as proud as it liked. "How little she knows, how little she knows!" the girl cried to herself; for what did that show after all but that Captain Everard's telegraphic confidant was Captain Everard's charming secret? Our young friend's perusal of her ladyship's telegram was literally prolonged by a momentary daze: what swam between her and the words, making her see them as through rippled shallow sunshot water, was the great, the perpetual flood of "How much I know—how much I know!" This produced a delay in her catching that, on the face, these words didn't give her what she wanted, though she was prompt enough with her remembrance that her grasp was, half the time, just of what was not on the face. "Miss Dolman, Parade Lodge, Parade Terrace, Dover. Let him instantly know right one, Hôtel de France, Ostend. Make it seven nine four nine six one. Wire me alternative Burfield's."

• • •

The girl slowly counted. Then he was at Ostend. This hooked on with so sharp a click that, not to feel she was as quickly letting it all slip from her, she had absolutely to hold it a minute longer and to do something to that end. Thus it was that she did on this occasion what she never did—threw off a "Reply paid?" that sounded officious, but that she partly made up for by deliberately affixing the stamps and by waiting till she had done so to give change. She had, for so much coolness, the strength that she considered she knew all about Miss Dolman.

"Yes—paid." She saw all sorts of things in this reply, even to a small suppressed start of surprise at so correct an assumption; even to an attempt the next minute at a fresh air of detachment. "How much, with the answer?" The calculation was not abstruse, but our intense observer required a moment more to make it, and this gave her ladyship time for a second thought. "Oh just wait!" The white begemmed hand bared to write rose in sudden nervousness to the side of the wonderful face which, with eyes of anxiety for the paper on the counter, she brought closer to the bars of the cage. "I think I must alter a word!" On this she recovered her telegram and looked over it again; but she had a new, an obvious trouble, and studied it without deciding and with much of the effect of making our young woman watch her.

This personage, meanwhile, at the sight of her expression, had decided on the spot. If she had always been sure they were in danger her ladyship's expression was the best possible sign of it. There was a word wrong, but she had lost the right one, and much clearly depended on her finding it again. The girl, therefore, sufficiently estimating the affluence of customers and the distraction of Mr. Buckton and the counter-clerk, took the jump and gave it. "Isn't it Cooper's?"

It was as if she had bodily leaped—cleared the top of the cage and alighted on her interlocutress. "Cooper's?"—the stare was heightened by a blush. Yes, she had made Juno blush.

This was all the greater reason for going on. "I mean instead of Burfield's."

Our young friend fairly pitied her; she had made her in an instant so helpless, and yet not a bit haughty nor outraged. She was only mystified and scared. "Oh, you know—?"

"Yes, I know!" Our young friend smiled, meeting the other's eyes, and, having made Juno blush, proceeded to patronise her. "I'll do it"—she put out a competent hand. Her ladyship only submitted, confused and bewildered, all presence of mind quite gone; and the next moment the telegram was in the cage again and its author out of the shop. Then quickly, boldly, under all the eyes that might have witnessed her tampering, the extraordinary little person at Cocker's made the proper change. People were really too giddy, and if they were, in a certain case, to be caught, it shouldn't be the fault of her own grand memory. Hadn't it been settled weeks before?—for Miss Dolman it was always to be "Cooper's."

CHAPTER XIV

But the summer "holidays" brought a marked difference; they were holidays for almost every one but the animals in the cage. The August days were flat and dry, and, with so little to feed it, she was conscious of the ebb of her interest in the secrets of the refined. She was in a position to follow the refined to the extent of knowing—they had made so many of their arrangements with her aid—exactly where they were; yet she felt quite as if the panorama had ceased unrolling and the band stopped playing. A stray member of the latter occasionally turned up, but the communications that passed before her bore now largely on rooms at hotels, prices of furnished houses, hours of trains, dates of sailings and arrangements for being "met"; she found them for the most part prosaic and coarse. The only thing was that they brought into her stuffy corner as straight a whiff of Alpine meadows and Scotch moors as she might hope ever to inhale; there were moreover in especial fat hot dull ladies who had out with her, to exasperation, the terms for seaside lodgings, which struck her as huge, and the matter of the number of beds required, which was not less portentous: this in reference to places of which the names—Eastbourne, Folkestone, Cromer, Scarborough, Whitby—tormented her with something of the sound of the plash of water that haunts the traveller in the desert. She had not been out of London for a dozen years, and the only thing to give a taste to the present dead weeks was the spice of a chronic resentment. The sparse customers, the people she did see, were the people who were "just off"—off on the decks of fluttered yachts, off to the uttermost point of rocky headlands where the very breeze was then playing for the want of which she said to herself that she sickened.

There was accordingly a sense in which, at such a period, the great differences of the human condition could press upon her more than ever; a circumstance drawing fresh force in truth from the very fact of the chance that at last, for a change, did squarely meet her—the chance to be "off," for a bit, almost as far as anybody. They took their turns in the cage as they took them both in the shop and at Chalk Farm; she had known these two months that time was to be allowed in September—no less than eleven days—for her personal private holiday. Much of her recent intercourse with Mr. Mudge had consisted of the hopes and fears, expressed mainly by himself, involved in the question of their getting the same dates—a question that, in proportion as the delight seemed assured, spread into a sea of speculation over the choice of where and how. All through July, on the Sunday evenings and at such other odd times as he could seize, he had flooded their talk with wild waves of calculation. It was practically settled that, with her mother, somewhere "on the south coast" (a phrase of which she liked the sound) they should put in their allowance together; but she already felt the prospect quite weary and worn with the way he went round and round on it. It had become his sole topic, the theme alike of his most solemn prudences and most placid jests, to which every opening led for return and revision and in which every little flower of a foretaste was pulled up as soon as planted. He had announced at the earliest day—characterising the whole business, from that moment, as their "plans," under which name he handled it as a Syndicate handles a Chinese or other Loan—he had promptly declared that the question must be thoroughly studied, and he produced, on the whole subject, from day to day, an amount of information that excited her wonder and even, not a little, as she frankly let him know, her disdain. When she thought of the danger in which another pair of lovers rapturously lived she enquired of him anew why he could leave nothing to chance. Then she got for answer that this profundity was just his pride, and he pitted Ramsgate against Bournemouth and even Boulogne against Jersey—for he had great ideas—with all the mastery of detail that was some day, professionally, to carry him afar.

The longer the time since she had seen Captain Everard the more she was booked, as she called it, to pass Park Chambers; and this was the sole amusement that in the lingering August days and the twilights sadly drawn out it was left her to cultivate. She had long since learned to know it for a feeble one, though its feebleness was perhaps scarce the reason for her saying to herself each evening as her time for departure approached: "No, no—not to-night." She never failed of that silent remark, any more than she failed of feeling, in some deeper place than she had even yet fully sounded, that one's remarks were as weak as straws and that, however one might indulge in them at eight o'clock, one's fate infallibly declared itself in absolute indifference to them at about eight-fifteen. Remarks were remarks, and very well for that; but fate was fate, and this young lady's was to pass Park Chambers every night in the working week. Out of the immensity of her knowledge of the life of the world there bloomed on these occasions as specific remembrance that it was regarded in that region, in August and September, as rather pleasant just to be caught for something or other in passing through town. Somebody was always passing and somebody might catch somebody else. It was in full cognisance of this subtle law that she adhered to the most ridiculous circuit she could have made to get home. One warm dull featureless Friday, when an accident had made her start from Cocker's a little later than usual, she became aware that something of which the infinite possibilities had for so long peopled her dreams was at last prodigiously upon her, though the perfection in which the conditions happened to present it was almost rich enough to be but the positive creation of a dream. She saw, straight before her, like a vista painted in a picture, the empty street and the lamps that burned pale in the dusk not yet established. It was into the convenience of this quiet twilight that a gentleman on the doorstep of the Chambers gazed with a vagueness that our young lady's little figure violently trembled, in the approach, with the measure of its power to dissipate. Everything indeed grew in a flash terrific and distinct; her old uncertainties fell away from her, and, since she was so familiar with fate, she felt as if the very nail that fixed it were driven in by the hard look with which, for a moment, Captain Everard awaited her.

The vestibule was open behind him and the porter as absent as on the day she had peeped in; he had just come out—was in town, in a tweed suit and a pot hat, but between two journeys—duly bored over his evening and at a loss what to do with it. Then it was that she was glad she had never met him in that way before: she reaped with such ecstasy the benefit of his not being able to think she passed often. She jumped in two seconds to the determination that he should even suppose it to be the very first time and the very oddest chance: this was while she still wondered if he would identify or notice her. His original attention had not, she instinctively knew, been for the young woman at Cocker's; it had only been for any young woman who might advance to the tune of her not troubling the quiet air, and in fact the poetic hour, with ugliness. Ah but then, and just as she had reached the door, came his second observation, a long light reach with which, visibly and quite amusedly, he recalled and placed her. They were on different sides, but the street, narrow and still, had only made more of a stage for the small momentary drama. It was not over, besides, it was far from over, even on his sending across the way, with the pleasantest laugh she had ever heard, a little lift of his hat and an "Oh good evening!" It was still less over on their meeting, the next minute, though rather indirectly and awkwardly, in the middle, of the road—a situation to which three or four steps of her own had unmistakeably contributed—and then passing not again to the side on which she had arrived, but back toward the portal of Park Chambers.

"I didn't know you at first. Are you taking a walk?"

"Ah I don't take walks at night! I'm going home after my work."

"Oh!"

That was practically what they had meanwhile smiled out, and his exclamation to which for a minute he appeared to have nothing to add, left them face to face and in just such an attitude as, for his part, he might have worn had he been wondering if he could properly ask her to come in. During this interval in fact she really felt his question to be just "How properly—?" It was simply a question of the degree of properness.

CHAPTER XV

She never knew afterwards quite what she had done to settle it, and at the time she only knew that they presently moved, with vagueness, yet with continuity, away from the picture of the lighted vestibule and the quiet stairs and well up the street together. This also must have been in the absence of a definite permission, of anything vulgarly articulate, for that matter, on the part of either; and it was to be, later on, a thing of remembrance and reflexion for her that the limit of what just here for a longish minute passed between them was his taking in her thoroughly successful deprecation, though conveyed without pride or sound or touch, of the idea that she might be, out of the cage, the very shop-girl at large that she hugged the theory she wasn't. Yes, it was strange, she afterwards thought, that so much could have come and gone and yet not disfigured the dear little intense crisis either with impertinence or with resentment, with any of the horrid notes of that kind of acquaintance. He had taken no liberty, as she would have so called it; and, through not having to betray the sense of one, she herself had, still more charmingly, taken none. On the spot, nevertheless, she could speculate as to what it meant that, if his relation with Lady Bradeen continued to be what her mind had built it up to, he should feel free to proceed with marked independence. This was one of the questions he was to leave her to deal with—the question whether people of his sort still asked girls up to their rooms when they were so awfully in love with other women. Could people of his sort do that without what people of her sort would call being "false to their love"? She had already a vision of how the true answer was that people of her sort didn't, in such cases, matter—didn't count as infidelity, counted only as something else: she might have been curious, since it came to that, to see exactly what.

Strolling together slowly in their summer twilight and their empty corner of Mayfair, they found themselves emerge at last opposite to one of the smaller gates of the Park; upon which, without any particular word about it—they were talking so of other things—

they crossed the street and went in and sat down on a bench. She had gathered by this time one magnificent hope about him—the hope he would say nothing vulgar. She knew thoroughly what she meant by that; she meant something quite apart from any matter of his being "false." Their bench was not far within; it was near the Park Lane paling and the patchy lamplight and the rumbling cabs and 'buses. A strange emotion had come to her, and she felt indeed excitement within excitement; above all a conscious joy in testing him with chances he didn't take. She had an intense desire he should know the type she really conformed to without her doing anything so low as tell him, and he had surely begun to know it from the moment he didn't seize the opportunities into which a common man would promptly have blundered. These were on the mere awkward surface, and their relation was beautiful behind and below them. She had questioned so little on the way what they might be doing that as soon as they were seated she took straight hold of it. Her hours, her confinement, the many conditions of service in the post-office, had—with a glance at his own postal resources and alternatives—formed, up to this stage, the subject of their talk. "Well, here we are, and it may be right enough; but this isn't the least, you know, where I was going."

"You were going home?"

"Yes, and I was already rather late. I was going to my supper."

"You haven't had it?"

"No indeed!"

"Then you haven't eaten—?"

He looked of a sudden so extravagantly concerned that she laughed out. "All day? Yes, we do feed once. But that was long ago. So I must presently say good-bye."

"Oh deary me!" he exclaimed with an intonation so droll and yet a touch so light and a distress so marked—a confession of helplessness for such a case, in short, so unrelieved—that she at once felt sure she had made the great difference plain. He looked at her with the kindest eyes and still without saying what she had known he wouldn't. She had known he wouldn't say "Then sup with me!" but the proof of it made her feel as if she had feasted.

"I'm not a bit hungry," she went on.

"Ah you must be, awfully!" he made answer, but settling himself on the bench as if, after all, that needn't interfere with his spending his evening. "I've always quite wanted the chance to thank you for the trouble you so often take for me."

"Yes, I know," she replied; uttering the words with a sense of the situation far deeper than any pretence of not fitting his allusion. She immediately felt him surprised and even a little puzzled at her frank assent; but for herself the trouble she had taken could only, in these fleeting minutes—they would probably never come back—be all there like a little hoard of gold in her lap. Certainly he might look at it, handle it, take up the pieces. Yet if he understood anything he must understand all. "I consider you've already immensely thanked me." The horror was back upon her of having seemed to hang about for some reward. "It's awfully odd you should have been there just the one time—!"

"The one time you've passed my place?"

"Yes; you can fancy I haven't many minutes to waste. There was a place to-night I had to stop at."

"I see, I see—" he knew already so much about her work. "It must be an awful grind—for a lady."

"It is, but I don't think I groan over it any more than my companions—and you've seen they're not ladies!" She mildly jested, but with an intention. "One gets used to things, and there are employments I should have hated much more." She had the finest conception of the beauty of not at least boring him. To whine, to count up her wrongs, was what a barmaid or a shop-girl would do, and it was quite enough to sit there like one of these.

"If you had had another employment," he remarked after a moment, "we might never have become acquainted."

"It's highly probable—and certainly not in the same way." Then, still with her heap of gold in her lap and something of the pride of it in her manner of holding her head, she continued not to move—she only smiled at him. The evening had thickened now; the scattered lamps were red; the Park, all before them, was full of obscure and ambiguous life; there were other couples on other benches whom it was impossible not to see, yet at whom it was impossible to look. "But I've walked so much out of my way with you only just to show you that—that"—with this she paused; it was not after all so easy to express—"that anything you may have thought is perfectly true."

"Oh I've thought a tremendous lot!" her companion laughed. "Do you mind my smoking?"

"Why should I? You always smoke there."

"At your place? Oh yes, but here it's different."

"No," she said as he lighted a cigarette, "that's just what it isn't. It's quite the same."

"Well, then, that's because 'there' it's so wonderful!"

"Then you're conscious of how wonderful it is?" she returned.

He jerked his handsome head in literal protest at a doubt. "Why that's exactly what I mean by my gratitude for all your trouble. It has been just as if you took a particular interest." She only looked at him by way of answer in such sudden headlong embarrassment, as she was quite aware, that while she remained silent he showed himself checked by her expression. "You have—haven't you?—taken a particular interest?"

"Oh a particular interest!" she quavered out, feeling the whole thing—her headlong embarrassment—get terribly the better of her, and wishing, with a sudden scare, all the more to keep her emotion down. She maintained her fixed smile a moment and turned her eyes over the peopled darkness, unconfused now, because there was something much more confusing. This, with a fatal great rush, was simply the fact that they were thus together. They were near, near, and all she had imagined of that had only become more true, more dreadful and overwhelming. She stared straight away in silence till she felt she looked an idiot; then, to say something, to say nothing, she attempted a sound which ended in a flood of tears.

CHAPTER XVI

Her tears helped her really to dissimulate, for she had instantly, in so public a situation, to recover herself. They had come and gone in half a minute, and she immediately explained them. "It's only because I'm tired. It's that—it's that!" Then she added a trifle incoherently: "I shall never see you again."

"Ah but why not?" The mere tone in which her companion asked this satisfied her once for all as to the amount of imagination for which she could count on him. It was naturally not large: it had exhausted itself in having arrived at what he had already touched upon—the sense of an intention in her poor zeal at Cocker's. But any deficiency of this kind was no fault in him: he wasn't obliged to have an inferior cleverness—to have second-rate resources and virtues. It had been as if he almost really believed she had simply cried for fatigue, and he accordingly put in some kind confused plea—"You ought really to take something: won't you have something or other somewhere?" to which she had made no response but a headshake of a sharpness that settled it. "Why shan't we all the more keep meeting?"

"I mean meeting this way—only this way. At my place there—that I've nothing to do with, and I hope of course you'll turn up, with your correspondence, when it suits you. Whether I stay or not, I mean; for I shall probably not stay."

"You're going somewhere else?" he put it with positive anxiety.

"Yes, ever so far away—to the other end of London. There are all sorts of reasons I can't tell you; and it's practically settled. It's better for me, much; and I've only kept on at Cocker's for you."

"For me?"

Making out in the dusk that he fairly blushed, she now measured how far he had been from knowing too much. Too much, she called it at present; and that was easy, since it proved so abundantly enough for her that he should simply be where he was. "As we shall never talk this way but to-night—never, never again!—here it all is. I'll say it; I don't care what you think; it doesn't matter; I only want to help you. Besides, you're kind—you're kind. I've been thinking then of leaving for ever so long. But you've come so often—at times—and you've had so much to do, and it has been so pleasant and interesting, that I've remained, I've kept putting off any change. More than once, when I had nearly decided, you've turned up again and I've thought 'Oh no!' That's the simple fact!" She had by this time got her confusion down so completely that she could laugh.

"This is what I meant when I said to you just now that I 'knew.' I've known perfectly that you knew I took trouble for you; and that knowledge has been for me, and I seemed to see it was for you, as if there were something—I don't know what to call it!—between us. I mean something unusual and good and awfully nice—something not a bit horrid or vulgar."

She had by this time, she could see, produced a great effect on him; but she would have spoken the truth to herself had she at the same moment declared that she didn't in the least care: all the more that the effect must be one of extreme perplexity. What, in it all, was visibly clear for him, none the less, was that he was tremendously glad he had met her. She held him, and he was astonished at the force of it; he was intent, immensely considerate. His elbow was on the back of the seat, and his head, with the pot-hat pushed quite back, in a boyish way, so that she really saw almost for the first time his forehead and hair, rested on the hand into which he had crumpled his gloves. "Yes," he assented, "it's not a bit horrid or vulgar."

She just hung fire a moment, then she brought out the whole truth. "I'd do anything for you. I'd do anything for you." Never in her life had she known anything so high and fine as this, just letting him have it and bravely and magnificently leaving it. Didn't the place, the associations and circumstances, perfectly make it sound what it wasn't? and wasn't that exactly the beauty?

So she bravely and magnificently left it, and little by little she felt him take it up, take it down, as if they had been on a satin sofa in a boudoir. She had never seen a boudoir, but there had been lots of boudoirs in the telegrams. What she had said at all events sank into him, so that after a minute he simply made a movement that had the result of placing his hand on her own—presently indeed that of her feeling herself firmly enough grasped. There was no pressure she need return, there was none she need decline; she just sat admirably still, satisfied for the time with the surprise and bewilderment of the impression she made on him. His agitation was even greater on the whole than she had at first allowed for. "I say, you know, you mustn't think of leaving!" he at last broke out.

"Of leaving Cocker's, you mean?"

"Yes, you must stay on there, whatever happens, and help a fellow."

She was silent a little, partly because it was so strange and exquisite to feel him watch her as if it really mattered to him and he were almost in suspense. "Then you have quite recognised what I've tried to do?" she asked.

"Why, wasn't that exactly what I dashed over from my door just now to thank you for?"

"Yes; so you said."

"And don't you believe it?"

She looked down a moment at his hand, which continued to cover her own; whereupon he presently drew it back, rather restlessly folding his arms. Without answering his question she went on: "Have you ever spoken of me?"

"Spoken of you?"

"Of my being there—of my knowing, and that sort of thing."

"Oh never to a human creature!" he eagerly declared.

She had a small drop at this, which was expressed in another pause, and she then returned to what he had just asked her. "Oh yes, I quite believe you like it—my always being there and our taking things up so familiarly and successfully: if not exactly where we left them," she laughed, "almost always at least at an interesting point!" He was about to say something in reply to this, but her friendly gaiety was quicker. "You want a great many things in life, a great many comforts and helps and luxuries—you want everything as pleasant as possible. Therefore, so far as it's in the power of any particular person to contribute to all that—" She had turned her face to him smiling, just thinking.

"Oh see here!" But he was highly amused. "Well, what then?" he enquired as if to humour her.

"Why the particular person must never fail. We must manage it for you somehow."

He threw back his head, laughing out; he was really exhilarated. "Oh yes, somehow!"

"Well, I think we each do—don't we?—in one little way and another and according to our limited lights. I'm pleased at any rate, for myself, that you are; for I assure you I've done my best."

"You do better than any one!" He had struck a match for another cigarette, and the flame lighted an instant his responsive finished face, magnifying into a pleasant grimace the kindness with which he paid her this tribute. "You're awfully clever, you know; cleverer, cleverer, cleverer—!" He had appeared on the point of making some tremendous statement; then suddenly, puffing his cigarette and shifting almost with violence on his seat, he let it altogether fall.

CHAPTER XVII

In spite of this drop, if not just by reason of it, she felt as if Lady Bradeen, all but named out, had popped straight up; and she practically betrayed her consciousness by waiting a little before she rejoined: "Cleverer than who?"

"Well, if I wasn't afraid you'd think I swagger, I should say—than anybody! If you leave your place there, where shall you go?" he more gravely asked.

"Oh too far for you ever to find me!"

"I'd find you anywhere."

The tone of this was so still more serious that she had but her one acknowledgement. "I'd do anything for you—I'd do anything for you," she repeated. She had already, she felt, said it all; so what did anything more, anything less, matter? That was the very reason indeed why she could, with a lighter note, ease him generously of any awkwardness produced by solemnity, either his own or hers. "Of course it must be nice for you to be able to think there are people all about who feel in such a way."

In immediate appreciation of this, however, he only smoked without looking at her. "But you don't want to give up your present work?" he at last threw out. "I mean you will stay in the post-office?"

"Oh yes; I think I've a genius for that."

"Rather! No one can touch you." With this he turned more to her again. "But you can get, with a move, greater advantages?"

"I can get in the suburbs cheaper lodgings. I live with my mother. We need some space. There's a particular place that has other inducements."

He just hesitated. "Where is it?"

"Oh quite out of your way. You'd never have time."

"But I tell you I'd go anywhere. Don't you believe it?"

"Yes, for once or twice. But you'd soon see it wouldn't do for you."

He smoked and considered; seemed to stretch himself a little and, with his legs out, surrender himself comfortably. "Well, well, well—I believe everything you say. I take it from you—anything you like—in the most extraordinary way." It struck her certainly—and almost without bitterness—that the way in which she was already, as if she had been an old friend, arranging for him and preparing the only magnificence she could muster, was quite the most extraordinary. "Don't, don't go!" he presently went on. "I shall miss you too horribly!"

"So that you just put it to me as a definite request?"—oh how she tried to divest this of all sound of the hardness of bargaining! That ought to have been easy enough, for what was she arranging to get? Before he could answer she had continued: "To be perfectly fair I should tell you I recognise at Cocker's certain strong attractions. All you people come. I like all the horrors."

"The horrors?"

"Those you all—you know the set I mean, your set—show me with as good a conscience as if I had no more feeling than a letter-box."

He looked quite excited at the way she put it. "Oh they don't know!"

"Don't know I'm not stupid? No, how should they?"

"Yes, how should they?" said the Captain sympathetically. "But isn't 'horrors' rather strong?"

"What you do is rather strong!" the girl promptly returned.

"What I do?"

"Your extravagance, your selfishness, your immorality, your crimes," she pursued, without heeding his expression.

"I say!"—her companion showed the queerest stare.

"I like them, as I tell you—I revel in them. But we needn't go into that," she quietly went on; "for all I get out of it is the harmless pleasure of knowing. I know, I know, I know!"—she breathed it ever so gently.

"Yes; that's what has been between us," he answered much more simply.

She could enjoy his simplicity in silence, and for a moment she did so. "If I do stay because you want it—and I'm rather capable of that—there are two or three things I think you ought to remember. One is, you know, that I'm there sometimes for days and weeks together without your ever coming."

"Oh I'll come every day!" he honestly cried.

She was on the point, at this, of imitating with her hand his movement of shortly before; but she checked herself, and there was no want of effect in her soothing substitute. "How can you? How can you?" He had, too manifestly, only to look at it there, in the vulgarly animated gloom, to see that he couldn't; and at this point, by the mere action of his silence, everything they had so definitely not named, the whole presence round which they had been circling, became part of their reference, settled in solidly between them. It was as if then for a minute they sat and saw it all in each other's eyes, saw so much that there was no need of a pretext for sounding it at last. "Your danger, your danger—!" Her voice indeed trembled with it, and she could only for the moment again leave it so.

During this moment he leaned back on the bench, meeting her in silence and with a face that grew more strange. It grew so strange that after a further instant she got straight up. She stood there as if their talk were now over, and he just sat and watched her. It was as if now—owing to the third person they had brought in—they must be more careful; so that the most he could finally say was: "That's where it is!"

"That's where it is!" the girl as guardedly replied. He sat still, and she added: "I won't give you up. Good-bye."

"Good-bye?"—he appealed, but without moving.

"I don't quite see my way, but I won't give you up," she repeated. "There. Good-bye."

It brought him with a jerk to his feet, tossing away his cigarette. His poor face was flushed. "See here—see here!"

"No, I won't; but I must leave you now," she went on as if not hearing him.

"See here—see here!" He tried, from the bench, to take her hand again.

But that definitely settled it for her: this would, after all, be as bad as his asking her to supper. "You mustn't come with me—no, no!"

He sank back, quite blank, as if she had pushed him. "I mayn't see you home?"

"No, no; let me go." He looked almost as if she had struck him, but she didn't care; and the manner in which she spoke—it was literally as if she were angry—had the force of a command. "Stay where you are!"

"See here—see here!" he nevertheless pleaded.

"I won't give you up!" she cried once more—this time quite with passion; on which she got away from him as fast as she could and left him staring after her.

CHAPTER XVIII

Mr. Mudge had lately been so occupied with their famous "plans" that he had neglected for a while the question of her transfer; but down at Bournemouth, which had found itself selected as the field of their recreation by a process consisting, it seemed, exclusively of innumerable pages of the neatest arithmetic in a very greasy but most orderly little pocket-book, the distracting possible melted away—the fleeting absolute ruled the scene. The plans, hour by hour, were simply superseded, and it was much of a rest to the girl, as she sat on the pier and overlooked the sea and the company, to see them evaporate in rosy fumes and to feel that from moment to moment there was less left to cipher about. The week proves blissfully fine, and her mother, at their lodgings—partly to her embarrassment and partly to her relief—struck up with the landlady an alliance that left the younger couple a great deal of freedom. This relative took her pleasure of a week at Bournemouth in a stuffy back-kitchen and endless talks; to that degree even that Mr. Mudge himself—habitually inclined indeed to a scrutiny of all mysteries and to seeing, as he sometimes admitted, too much in things—made remarks on it as he sat on the cliff with his betrothed, or on the decks of steamers that conveyed them, close-packed items in terrific totals of enjoyment, to the Isle of Wight and the Dorset coast.

He had a lodging in another house, where he had speedily learned the importance of keeping his eyes open, and he made no secret of his suspecting that sinister mutual connivances might spring, under the roof of his companions, from unnatural sociabilities. At the same time he fully recognised that as a source of anxiety, not to say of expense, his future mother-in law would have weighted them more by accompanying their steps than by giving her hostess, in the interest of the tendency they considered that they never mentioned, equivalent pledges as to the tea-caddy and the jam-pot. These were the questions—these indeed the familiar commodities—that he had now to put into the scales; and his betrothed had in consequence, during her holiday, the odd and yet pleasant and almost languid sense of an anticlimax. She had become conscious of an extraordinary collapse, a surrender to stillness and to retrospect. She cared neither to walk nor to sail; it was enough for her to sit on benches and wonder at the sea and taste the air and not be at Cocker's and not see the counter-clerk. She still seemed to wait for something—something in the key of the immense discussions that had mapped out their little week of idleness on the scale of a world-atlas. Something came at last, but without perhaps appearing quite adequately to crown the monument.

Preparation and precaution were, however, the natural flowers of Mr. Mudge's mind, and in proportion as these things declined in one quarter they inevitably bloomed elsewhere. He could always, at the worst, have on Tuesday the project of their taking the Swanage boat on Thursday, and on Thursday that of their ordering minced kidneys on Saturday. He had moreover a constant gift of inexorable enquiry as to where and what they should have gone and have done if they hadn't been exactly as they were. He had in short his resources, and his mistress had never been so conscious of them; on the other hand they never interfered so little with her own. She liked to be as she was—if it could only have lasted. She could accept even without bitterness a rigour of economy so great that the little fee they paid for admission to the pier had to be balanced against other delights. The people at Ladle's and at Thrupp's had their ways of amusing themselves, whereas she had to sit and hear Mr. Mudge talk of what he might do if he didn't take a bath, or of the bath he might take if he only hadn't taken something else. He was always with her now, of course, always beside her; she saw him more than "hourly," more than ever yet, more even than he had planned she should do at Chalk Farm. She preferred to sit at the far end, away from the band and the crowd; as to which she had frequent differences with her friend, who reminded her often that they could have only in the thick of it the sense of the money they were getting back. That had little effect on her, for she got back her money by seeing many things, the things of the past year, fall together and connect themselves, undergo the happy relegation that transforms melancholy and misery, passion and effort, into experience and knowledge.

She liked having done with them, as she assured herself she had practically done, and the strange thing was that she neither missed the procession now nor wished to keep her place for it. It had become there, in the sun and the breeze and the sea-smell, a far-away story, a picture of another life. If Mr. Mudge himself liked processions, liked them at Bournemouth and on the pier quite as much as at Chalk Farm or anywhere, she learned after a little not to be worried by his perpetual counting of the figures that made them up. There were dreadful women in particular, usually fat and in men's caps and write shoes, whom he could never let alone—not that she cared; it was not the great world, the world of Cocker's and Ladle's and Thrupp's, but it offered an endless field to his faculties of memory, philosophy, and frolic. She had never accepted him so much, never arranged so successfully for making him chatter while she carried on secret conversations. This separate commerce was with herself; and if they both practised a great thrift she had quite mastered that of merely spending words enough to keep him imperturbably and continuously going.

He was charmed with the panorama, not knowing—or at any rate not at all showing that he knew—what far other images peopled her mind than the women in the navy caps and the shop-boys in the blazers. His observations on these types, his general interpretation of the show, brought home to her the prospect of Chalk Farm. She wondered sometimes that he should have derived so little illumination, during his period, from the society at Cocker's. But one evening while their holiday cloudlessly waned he gave her such a proof of his quality as might have made her ashamed of her many suppressions. He brought out something that, in all his overflow, he had been able to keep back till other matters were disposed of. It was the announcement that he was at last ready to marry—that he saw his way. A rise at Chalk Farm had been offered him; he was to be taken into the business, bringing with him a capital the estimation of which by other parties constituted the handsomest recognition yet made of the head on his shoulders. Therefore their waiting was over—it could be a question of a near date. They would settle this date before going back, and he meanwhile had his eye on a sweet little home. He would take her to see it on their first Sunday.

CHAPTER XIX

His having kept this great news for the last, having had such a card up his sleeve and not floated it out in the current of his chatter and the luxury of their leisure, was one of those incalculable strokes by which he could still affect her; the kind of thing that reminded her of the latent force that had ejected the drunken soldier—an example of the profundity of which his promotion was the proof. She listened a while in silence, on this occasion, to the wafted strains of the music; she took it in as she had not quite done before that her future was now constituted. Mr. Mudge was distinctly her fate; yet at this moment she turned her face quite away from him, showing him so long a mere quarter of her cheek that she at last again heard his voice. He couldn't see a pair of tears that were partly the reason of her delay to give him the assurance he required; but he expressed at a venture the hope that she had had her fill of Cocker's.

She was finally able to turn back. "Oh quite. There's nothing going on. No one comes but the Americans at Thrupp's, and they don't do much. They don't seem to have a secret in the world."

"Then the extraordinary reason you've been giving me for holding on there has ceased to work?"

She thought a moment. "Yes, that one. I've seen the thing through—I've got them all in my pocket."

"So you're ready to come?"

For a little again she made no answer. "No, not yet, all the same. I've still got a reason—a different one."

He looked her all over as if it might have been something she kept in her mouth or her glove or under her jacket—something she was even sitting upon. "Well, I'll have it, please."

"I went out the other night and sat in the Park with a gentleman," she said at last.

Nothing was ever seen like his confidence in her and she wondered a little now why it didn't irritate her. It only gave her ease and space, as she felt, for telling him the whole truth that no one knew. It had arrived at present at her really wanting to do that, and yet to do it not in the least for Mr. Mudge, but altogether and only for herself. This truth filled out for her there the whole experience about to relinquish, suffused and coloured it as a picture that she should keep and that, describe it as she might, no one but herself would ever really see. Moreover she had no desire whatever to make Mr. Mudge jealous; there would be no amusement in it, for the amusement she had lately known had spoiled her for lower pleasures. There were even no materials for it. The odd thing was how she never doubted that, properly handled, his passion was poisonable; what had happened was that he had cannily selected a partner with no poison to distil. She read then and there that she should never interest herself in anybody as to whom some other sentiment, some superior view, wouldn't be sure to interfere for him with jealousy. "And what did you get out of that?" he asked with a concern that was not in the least for his honour.

"Nothing but a good chance to promise him I wouldn't forsake him. He's one of my customers."

"Then it's for him not to forsake you."

"Well, he won't. It's all right. But I must just keep on as long as he may want me."

"Want you to sit with him in the Park?"

"He may want me for that—but I shan't. I rather liked it, but once, under the circumstances, is enough. I can do better for him in another manner."

"And what manner, pray?"

"Well, elsewhere."

"Elsewhere?—I say!"

This was an ejaculation used also by Captain Everard, but oh with what a different sound! "You needn't 'say'—there's nothing to be said. And yet you ought perhaps to know."

"Certainly I ought. But what—up to now?"

"Why exactly what I told him. That I'd do anything for him."

"What do you mean by 'anything'?"

"Everything."

Mr. Mudge's immediate comment on this statement was to draw from his pocket a crumpled paper containing the remains of half a pound of "sundries." These sundries had figured conspicuously in his prospective sketch of their tour, but it was only at the end of three days that they had defined themselves unmistakeably as chocolate-creams. "Have another?—that one," he said. She had another, but not the one he indicated, and then he continued: "What took place afterwards?"

"Afterwards?"

"What did you do when you had told him you'd do everything?"

"I simply came away."

"Out of the Park?"

"Yes, leaving him there. I didn't let him follow me."

"Then what did you let him do?"

"I didn't let him do anything."

Mr. Mudge considered an instant. "Then what did you go there for?" His tone was even slightly critical.

"I didn't quite know at the time. It was simply to be with him, I suppose—just once. He's in danger, and I wanted him to know I know it. It makes meeting him—at Cocker's, since it's that I want to stay on for—more interesting."

"It makes it mighty interesting for me!" Mr. Mudge freely declared. "Yet he didn't follow you?" he asked. "I would!"

"Yes, of course. That was the way you began, you know. You're awfully inferior to him."

"Well, my dear, you're not inferior to anybody. You've got a cheek! What's he in danger of?"

"Of being found out. He's in love with a lady—and it isn't right—and I've found him out."

"That'll be a look-out for me!" Mr. Mudge joked. "You mean she has a husband?"

"Never mind what she has! They're in awful danger, but his is the worst, because he's in danger from her too."

"Like me from you—the woman I love? If he's in the same funk as me—"

"He's in a worse one. He's not only afraid of the lady—he's afraid of other things."

Mr. Mudge selected another chocolate-cream. "Well, I'm only afraid of one! But how in the world can you help this party?"

"I don't know—perhaps not at all. But so long as there's a chance—"

"You won't come away?"

"No, you've got to wait for me."

Mr. Mudge enjoyed what was in his mouth. "And what will he give you?"

"Give me?"

"If you do help him."

"Nothing. Nothing in all the wide world."

"Then what will he give me?" Mr. Mudge enquired. "I mean for waiting."

The girl thought a moment; then she got up to walk. "He never heard of you," she replied.

"You haven't mentioned me?"

"We never mention anything. What I've told you is just what I've found out."

Mr. Mudge, who had remained on the bench, looked up at her; she often preferred to be quiet when he proposed to walk, but now that he seemed to wish to sit she had a desire to move. "But you haven't told me what he has found out."

She considered her lover. "He'd never find you, my dear!"

Her lover, still on his seat, appealed to her in something of the attitude in which she had last left Captain Everard, but the impression was not the same. "Then where do I come in?"

"You don't come in at all. That's just the beauty of it!"—and with this she turned to mingle with the multitude collected round the band. Mr. Mudge presently overtook her and drew her arm into his own with a quiet force that expressed the serenity of possession; in consonance with which it was only when they parted for the night at her door that he referred again to what she had told him.

"Have you seen him since?"

"Since the night in the Park? No, not once."

"Oh, what a cad!" said Mr. Mudge.

CHAPTER XX

It was not till the end of October that she saw Captain Everard again, and on that occasion—the only one of all the series on which hindrance had been so utter—no communication with him proved possible. She had made out even from the cage that it was a charming golden day: a patch of hazy autumn sunlight lay across the sanded floor and also, higher up, quickened into brightness a row of ruddy bottled syrups. Work was slack and the place in general empty; the town, as they said in the cage, had not waked up, and the feeling of the day likened itself to something than in happier conditions she would have thought of romantically as Saint Martin's summer. The counter-clerk had gone to his dinner; she herself was busy with arrears of postal jobs, in the midst of which she became aware that Captain Everard had apparently been in the shop a minute and that Mr. Buckton had already seized him.

He had as usual half a dozen telegrams; and when he saw that she saw him and their eyes met he gave, on bowing to her, an exaggerated laugh in which she read a new consciousness. It was a confession of awkwardness; it seemed to tell her that of course he knew he ought better to have kept his head, ought to have been clever enough to wait, on some pretext, till he should have found her free. Mr. Buckton was a long time with him, and her attention was soon demanded by other visitors; so that nothing passed between them but the fulness of their silence. The look she took from him was his greeting, and the other one a simple sign of the eyes sent her before going out. The only token they exchanged therefore was his tacit assent to her wish that since they couldn't attempt a certain frankness they should attempt nothing at all. This was her intense preference; she could be as still and cold as any one when that was the sole solution.

Yet more than any contact hitherto achieved these counted instants struck her as marking a step: they were built so—just in the mere flash—on the recognition of his now definitely knowing what it was she would do for him. The "anything, anything" she had uttered in the Park went to and fro between them and under the poked-out china that interposed. It had all at last even put on the air of their not needing now clumsily to manoeuvre to converse: their former little postal make-believes, the intense implications of questions and answers and change, had become in the light of the personal fact, of their having had their moment, a possibility comparatively poor. It was as if they had met for all time—it exerted on their being in presence again an influence so prodigious. When she watched herself, in the memory of that night, walk away from him as if she were making an end, she found something too pitiful in the primness of such a gait. Hadn't she precisely established on the part of each a consciousness that could end only with death?

It must be admitted that in spite of this brave margin an irritation, after he had gone, remained with her; a sense that presently became one with a still sharper hatred of Mr. Buckton, who, on her friend's withdrawal, had retired with the telegrams to the sounder and left her the other work. She knew indeed she should have a chance to see them, when she would, on file; and she was divided, as the day went on, between the two impressions of all that was lost and all that was re-asserted. What beset her above all, and as she had almost never known it before, was the desire to bound straight out, to overtake the autumn afternoon before it passed away for ever and hurry off to the Park and perhaps be with him there again on a bench. It became for an hour a fantastic vision with her that he might just have gone to sit and wait for her. She could almost hear him, through the tick of the sounder, scatter with his stick, in his impatience, the fallen leaves of October. Why should such a vision seize her at this particular moment with such a shake? There was a time—from four to five—when she could have cried with happiness and rage.

Business quickened, it seemed, toward five, as if the town did wake up; she had therefore more to do, and she went through it with little sharp stampings and jerkings: she made the crisp postal-orders fairly snap while she breathed to herself "It's the last day—the last day!" The last day of what? She couldn't have told. All she knew now was that if she were out of the cage she wouldn't in the least have minded, this time, its not yet being dark. She would have gone straight toward Park Chambers and have hung about there till no matter when. She would have waited, stayed, rung, asked, have gone in, sat on the stairs. What the day was the last of was probably, to her strained inner sense, the group of golden ones, of any occasion for seeing the hazy sunshine slant at that angle into the smelly shop, of any range of chances for his wishing still to repeat to her the two words she had in the Park scarcely let him bring out. "See here—see here!"— the sound of these two words had been with her perpetually; but it was in her ears to-day without mercy, with a loudness that grew and grew. What was it they then expressed? what was it he had wanted her to see? She seemed, whatever it was, perfectly to see it now—to see that if she should just chuck the whole thing, should have a great and beautiful courage, he would somehow make everything up to her. When the clock struck five she was on the very point of saying to Mr. Buckton that she was deadly ill and rapidly getting worse. This announcement was on her lips, and she had quite composed the pale hard face she would offer him: "I can't stop—I must go home. If I feel better, later on, I'll come back. I'm very sorry, but I must go." At that instant Captain Everard once more stood there, producing in her agitated spirit, by his real presence, the strangest, quickest revolution. He stopped her off without knowing it, and by the time he had been a minute in the shop she felt herself saved.

That was from the first minute how she thought of it. There were again other persons with whom she was occupied, and again the situation could only be expressed by their silence. It was expressed, of a truth, in a larger phrase than ever yet, for her eyes now spoke to him with a kind of supplication. "Be quiet, be quiet!" they pleaded; and they saw his own reply: "I'll do whatever you say; I won't even look at you—see,

see!" They kept conveying thus, with the friendliest liberality, that they wouldn't look, quite positively wouldn't. What she was to see was that he hovered at the other end of the counter, Mr. Buckton's end, and surrendered himself again to that frustration. It quickly proved so great indeed that what she was to see further was how he turned away before he was attended to, and hung off, waiting, smoking, looking about the shop; how he went over to Mr. Cocker's own counter and appeared to price things, gave in fact presently two or three orders and put down money, stood there a long time with his back to her, considerately abstaining from any glance round to see if she were free. It at last came to pass in this way that he had remained in the shop longer than she had ever yet known to do, and that, nevertheless, when he did turn about she could see him time himself—she was freshly taken up—and cross straight to her postal subordinate, whom some one else had released. He had in his hand all this while neither letters nor telegrams, and now that he was close to her—for she was close to the counter-clerk—it brought her heart into her mouth merely to see him look at her neighbour and open his lips. She was too nervous to bear it. He asked for a Post-Office Guide, and the young man whipped out a new one; whereupon he said he wished not to purchase, but only to consult one a moment; with which, the copy kept on loan being produced, he once more wandered off.

What was he doing to her? What did he want of her? Well, it was just the aggravation of his "See here!" She felt at this moment strangely and portentously afraid of him—had in her ears the hum of a sense that, should it come to that kind of tension, she must fly on the spot to Chalk Farm. Mixed with her dread and with her reflexion was the idea that, if he wanted her so much as he seemed to show, it might be after all simply to do for him the "anything" she had promised, the "everything" she had thought it so fine to bring out to Mr. Mudge. He might want her to help him, might have some particular appeal; though indeed his manner didn't denote that—denoted on the contrary an embarrassment, an indecision, something of a desire not so much to be helped as to be treated rather more nicely than she had treated him the other time. Yes, he considered quite probably that he had help rather to offer than to ask for. Still, none the less, when he again saw her free he continued to keep away from her; when he came back with his thumbed Guide it was Mr. Buckton he caught—it was from Mr. Buckton he obtained half-a-crown's-worth of stamps.

After asking for the stamps he asked, quite as a second thought, for a postal-order for ten shillings. What did he want with so many stamps when he wrote so few letters? How could he enclose a postal-order in a telegram? She expected him, the next thing, to go into the corner and make up one of his telegrams—half a dozen of them—on purpose to prolong his presence. She had so completely stopped looking at him that she could only guess his movements—guess even where his eyes rested. Finally she saw him make a dash that might have been toward the nook where the forms were hung; and at this she suddenly felt that she couldn't keep it up. The counter-clerk had just taken a telegram from a slavey, and, to give herself something to cover her, she snatched it out of his hand. The gesture was so violent that he gave her in return an odd look, and she also perceived that Mr. Buckton noticed it. The latter personage, with a quick stare at her, appeared for an instant to wonder whether his snatching it in his turn mightn't be the thing she would least like, and she anticipated this practical criticism by the frankest glare she had ever given him. It sufficed: this time it paralysed him; and she sought with her trophy the refuge of the sounder.

CHAPTER XXI

It was repeated the next day; it went on for three days; and at the end of that time she knew what to think. When, at the beginning, she had emerged from her temporary shelter Captain Everard had quitted the shop; and he had not come again that evening, as it had struck her he possibly might—might all the more easily that there were numberless persons who came, morning and afternoon, numberless times, so that he wouldn't necessarily have attracted attention. The second day it was different and yet on the whole worse. His access to her had become possible—she felt herself even reaping the fruit of her yesterday's glare at Mr. Buckton; but transacting his business with him didn't simplify—it could, in spite of the rigour of circumstance, feed so her new conviction. The rigour was tremendous, and his telegrams—not now mere pretexts for getting at her—were apparently genuine; yet the conviction had taken but a night to develop. It could be simply enough expressed; she had had the glimmer of it the day before in her idea that he needed no more help than she had already given; that it was help he himself was prepared to render. He had come up to town but for three or four days; he had been absolutely obliged to be absent after the other time; yet he would, now that he was face to face with her, stay on as much longer as she liked. Little by little it was thus clarified, though from the first flash of his re-appearance she had read into it the real essence.

That was what the night before, at eight o'clock, her hour to go, had made her hang back and dawdle. She did last things or pretended to do them; to be in the cage had suddenly become her safety, and she was literally afraid of the alternate self who might be waiting outside. He might be waiting; it was he who was her alternate self, and of him she was afraid. The most extraordinary change had taken place in her from the moment of her catching the impression he seemed to have returned on purpose to give her. Just before she had done so, on that bewitched afternoon, she had seen herself approach without a scruple the porter at Park Chambers; then as the effect of the rush of a consciousness quite altered she had on at last quitting Cocker's, gone straight home for the first time since her return from Bournemouth. She had passed his door every night for weeks, but nothing would have induced her to pass it now. This change was the tribute of her fear—the result of a change in himself as to which she needed no more explanation than his mere face vividly gave her; strange though it was to find an element of deterrence in the object that she regarded as the most beautiful in the world. He had taken it from her in the Park that night that she wanted him not to propose to her to sup; but he had put away the lesson by this time—he practically proposed supper every time he looked at her. This was what, for that matter, mainly filled the three days. He came in twice on each of these, and it was as if he came in to give her a chance to relent. That was after all, she said to herself in the intervals, the most that he did. There were ways, she fully recognised, in which he spared her, and other particular ways as to which she meant that her silence should be full to him of exquisite pleading. The most particular of all was his not being outside, at the corner, when she quitted the place for the night. This he might so easily have been—so easily if he hadn't been so nice. She continued to recognise in his forbearance the fruit of her dumb supplication, and the only compensation he found for it was the harmless freedom of being able to appear to say: "Yes, I'm in town only for three or four days, but, you know, I would stay on." He struck her as calling attention each day, each hour, to the rapid ebb of time; he exaggerated to the point of putting it that there were only two days more, that there was at last, dreadfully, only one.

There were other things still that he struck her as doing with a special intention; as to the most marked

of which—unless indeed it were the most obscure—
she might well have marvelled that it didn't seem to
her more horrid. It was either the frenzy of her imagination or the disorder of his baffled passion that gave
her once or twice the vision of his putting down redun-
dant money—sovereigns not concerned with the little
payments he was perpetually making—so that she
might give him some sign of helping him to slip them
over to her. What was most extraordinary in this impression was the amount of excuse that, with some incoherence, she found for him. He wanted to pay her
because there was nothing to pay her for. He wanted
to offer her things he knew she wouldn't take. He
wanted to show her how much he respected her by giving her the supreme chance to show him she was re-
spectable. Over the dryest transactions, at any rate,
their eyes had out these questions. On the third day he
put in a telegram that had evidently something of the
same point as the stray sovereigns—a message that
was in the first place concocted and that on a second
thought he took back from her before she had stamped
it. He had given her time to read it and had only then
bethought himself that he had better not send it. If it
was not to Lady Bradeen at Twindle—where she knew
her ladyship then to be—this was because an address
to Doctor Buzzard at Brickwood was just as good,
with the added merit of its not giving away quite so
much a person whom he had still, after all, in a manner
to consider. It was of course most complicated, only
half lighted; but there was, discernibly enough, a
scheme of communication in which Lady Bradeen at

Twindle and Dr. Buzzard at Brickwood were, within limits, one and the same person. The words he had shown her and then taken back consisted, at all events, of the brief but vivid phrase "Absolutely impossible." The point was not that she should transmit it; the point was just that she should see it. What was absolutely impossible was that before he had setted something at Cocker's he should go either to Twindle or to Brickwood.

The logic of this, in turn, for herself, was that she could lend herself to no settlement so long as she so intensely knew. What she knew was that he was, almost under peril of life, clenched in a situation: therefore how could she also know where a poor girl in the P.O. might really stand? It was more and more between them that if he might convey to her he was free, with all the impossible locked away into a closed chapter, her own case might become different for her, she might understand and meet him and listen. But he could convey nothing of the sort, and he only fidgeted and floundered in his want of power. The chapter wasn't in the least closed, not for the other party; and the other party had a pull, somehow and somewhere: this his whole attitude and expression confessed, at the same time that they entreated her not to remember and not to mind. So long as she did remember and did mind he could only circle about and go and come, doing futile things of which he was ashamed.

He was ashamed of his two words to Dr. Buzzard; he went out of the shop as soon as he had crumpled up the paper again and thrust it into his pocket. It had been an abject little exposure of dreadful impossible passion. He appeared in fact to be too ashamed to come back. He had once more left town, and a first week elapsed, and a second. He had had naturally to return to the real mistress of his fate; she had insisted—she knew how to insist, and he couldn't put in another hour. There was always a day when she called time. It was known to our young friend moreover that he had now been dispatching telegrams from other offices. She knew at last so much that she had quite lost her earlier sense of merely guessing. There were no different shades of distinctness—it all bounced out.

CHAPTER XXII

Eighteen days elapsed, and she had begun to think it probable she should never see him again. He too then understood now: he had made out that she had secrets and reasons and impediments, that even a poor girl at the P.O. might have her complications. With the charm she had cast on him lightened by distance he had suffered a final delicacy to speak to him, had made up his mind that it would be only decent to let her alone. Never so much as during these latter days had she felt the precariousness of their relation—the happy beautiful untroubled original one, if it could only have been restored—in which the public servant and the casual public only were concerned. It hung at the best by the merest silken thread, which was at the mercy of any accident and might snap at any minute. She arrived by the end of the fortnight at the highest sense of actual fitness, never doubting that her decision was now complete. She would just give him a few days more to come back to her on a proper impersonal basis—for even to an embarrassing representative of the casual public a public servant with a conscience did owe something—and then would signify to Mr. Mudge that she was ready for the little home. It had been visited, in the further talk she had had with him at Bournemouth, from garret to cellar, and they had especially lingered, with their respectively darkened brows, before the niche into which it was to be broached to her mother that she must find means to fit.

He had put it to her more definitely than before that his calculations had allowed for that dingy presence, and he had thereby marked the greatest impression he had ever made on her. It was a stroke superior even again to his handling of the drunken soldier. What she considered that in the face of it she hung on at Cocker's for was something she could only have described as the common fairness of a last word. Her actual last word had been, till it should be superseded, that she wouldn't forsake her other friend, and it stuck to her through thick and thin that she was still at her post and on her honour. This other friend had shown so much beauty of conduct already that he would surely after all just re-appear long enough to relieve her, to give her something she could take away. She saw it, caught it, at times, his parting present; and there were moments when she felt herself sitting like a beggar with a hand held out to almsgiver who only fumbled. She hadn't taken the sovereigns, but she would take the penny. She heard, in imagination, on the counter, the ring of the copper. "Don't put yourself out any longer," he would say, "for so bad a case. You've done all there is to be done. I thank and acquit and release you. Our lives take us. I don't know much—though I've really been interested—about yours, but I suppose you've got one. Mine at any rate will take me—and where it will. Heigh-ho! Good-bye." And then once more, for the sweetest faintest flower of all: "Only, I say—see here!" She had framed the whole picture with a squareness that included also the image of how again she would decline to "see there," decline, as she might say, to see anywhere, see anything. Yet it befell that just in the fury of this escape she saw more than ever.

He came back one night with a rush, near the moment of their closing, and showed her a face so different and new, so upset and anxious, that almost anything seemed to look out of it but clear recognition. He poked in a telegram very much as if the simple sense of pressure, the distress of extreme haste, had blurred the remembrance of where in particular he was. But as she met his eyes a light came; it broke indeed on the spot into a positive conscious glare. That made up for everything, since it was an instant proclamation of the celebrated "danger"; it seemed to pour things out in a flood. "Oh yes, here it is—it's upon me at last! Forget, for God's sake, my having worried or bored you, and just help me, just save me, by getting this off without the loss of a second!" Something grave had clearly occurred, a crisis declared itself. She recognised immediately the person to whom the telegram was addressed—the Miss Dolman of Parade Lodge to whom Lady Bradeen had wired, at Dover, on the last occasion, and whom she had then, with her recollection of previous arrangements, fitted into a particular setting. Miss Dolman had figured before and not figured since, but she was now the subject of an imperative appeal. "Absolutely necessary to see you. Take last train Victoria if you can catch it. If not, earliest morning, and answer me direct either way."

"Reply paid?" said the girl. Mr. Buckton had just departed and the counter-clerk was at the sounder. There was no other representative of the public, and she had never yet, as it seemed to her, not even in the street or in the Park, been so alone with him.

"Oh yes, reply paid, and as sharp as possible, please."

She affixed the stamps in a flash. "She'll catch the train!" she then declared to him breathlessly, as if she could absolutely guarantee it.

"I don't know—I hope so. It's awfully important. So kind of you. Awfully sharp, please." It was wonderfully innocent now, his oblivion of all but his danger. Anything else that had ever passed between them was utterly out of it. Well, she had wanted him to be impersonal!

There was less of the same need therefore, happily, for herself; yet she only took time, before she flew to the sounder, to gasp at him: "You're in trouble?"

"Horrid, horrid—there's a row!" But they parted, on it, in the next breath; and as she dashed at the sounder, almost pushing, in her violence, the counter-clerk off the stool, she caught the bang with which, at Cocker's door, in his further precipitation, he closed the apron of the cab into which he had leaped. As he rebounded to some other precaution suggested by his alarm, his appeal to Miss Dolman flashed straight away.

But she had not, on the morrow, been in the place five minutes before he was with her again, still more discomposed and quite, now, as she said to herself, like a frightened child coming to its mother. Her companions were there, and she felt it to be emarkable how, in the presence of his agitation, his mere scared exposed nature, she suddenly ceased to mind. It came to her as it had never come to her before that with absolute directness and assurance they might carry almost anything off. He had nothing to send—she was sure he had been wiring all over—and yet his business was evidently huge. There was nothing but that in his eyes—not a glimmer of reference or memory. He was almost haggard with anxiety and had clearly not slept a wink. Her pity for him would have given her any courage, and she seemed to know at last why she had been such a fool. "She didn't come?" she panted.

"Oh yes, she came; but there has been some mistake. We want a telegram."

"A telegram?"

"One that was sent from here ever so long ago. There was something in it that has to be recovered. Something very, very important, please—we want it immediately."

He really spoke to her as if she had been some strange young woman at Knightsbridge or Paddington; but it had no other effect on her than to give her the measure of his tremendous flurry. Then it was that, above all, she felt how much she had missed in the gaps and blanks and absent answers—how much she had had to dispense with: it was now black darkness save for this little wild red flare. So much as that she saw, so much her mind dealt with. One of the lovers was quaking somewhere out of town, and the other was quaking just where he stood. This was vivid enough, and after an instant she knew it was all she wanted. She wanted no detail, no fact—she wanted no nearer vision of discovery or shame. "When was your telegram? Do you mean you sent it from here?" She tried to do the young woman at Knightsbridge.

"Oh yes, from here—several weeks ago. Five, six, seven"—he was confused and impatient—"don't you remember?"

"Remember?" she could scarcely keep out of her face, at the word, the strangest of smiles.

But the way he didn't catch what it meant was perhaps even stranger still. "I mean, don't you keep the old ones?"

"For a certain time."

"But how long?"

She thought; she must do the young woman, and she knew exactly what the young woman would say and, still more, wouldn't. "Can you give me the date?"

"Oh God, no! It was some time or other in August—toward the end. It was to the same address as the one I gave you last night."

"Oh!" said the girl, knowing at this the deepest thrill she had ever felt. It came to her there, with her eyes on his face, that she held the whole thing in her hand, held it as she held her pencil, which might have broken at that instant in her tightened grip. This made her feel like the very fountain of fate, but the emotion was such a flood that she had to press it back with all her force. That was positively the reason, again, of her flute-like Paddington tone. "You can't give us anything a little nearer?" Her "little" and her "us" came straight from Paddington. These things were no false note for him—his difficulty absorbed them all. The eyes with which he pressed her, and in the depths of which she read terror and rage and literal tears, were just the same he would have shown any other prim person.

"I don't know the date. I only know the thing went from here, and just about the time I speak of. It wasn't delivered, you see. We've got to recover it."

CHAPTER XXIII

She was as struck with the beauty of his plural pronoun as she had judged he might be with that of her own; but she knew now so well what she was about that she could almost play with him and with her new-born joy. "You say 'about the time you speak of.' But I don't think you speak of an exact time—do you?"

He looked splendidly helpless. "That's just what I want to find out. Don't you keep the old ones?—can't you look it up?"

Our young lady—still at Paddington—turned the question over. "It wasn't delivered?"

"Yes, it was; yet, at the same time, don't you know? it wasn't." He just hung back, but he brought it out. "I mean it was intercepted, don't you know? and there was something in it." He paused again and, as if to further his quest and woo and supplicate success and recovery, even smiled with an effort at the agreeable that was almost ghastly and that turned the knife in her tenderness. What must be the pain of it all, of the open gulf and the throbbing fever, when this was the mere hot breath? "We want to get what was in it—to know what it was."

"I see—I see." She managed just the accent they had at Paddington when they stared like dead fish. "And you have no clue?"

"Not at all—I've the clue I've just given you."

"Oh the last of August?" If she kept it up long enough she would make him really angry.

"Yes, and the address, as I've said."

"Oh the same as last night?"

He visibly quivered, as with a gleam of hope; but it only poured oil on her quietude, and she was still deliberate. She ranged some papers. "Won't you look?" he went on.

"I remember your coming," she replied.

He blinked with a new uneasiness; it might have begun to come to him, through her difference, that he was somehow different himself. "You were much quicker then, you know!"

"So were you—you must do me that justice," she answered with a smile. "But let me see. Wasn't it Dover?"

"Yes, Miss Dolman—"

"Parade Lodge, Parade Terrace?"

"Exactly—thank you so awfully much!" He began to hope again. "Then you have it—the other one?"

She hesitated afresh; she quite dangled him. "It was brought by a lady?"

"Yes; and she put in by mistake something wrong. That's what we've got to get hold of!" Heavens, what was he going to say?—flooding poor Paddington with wild betrayals! She couldn't too much, for her joy, dangle him, yet she couldn't either, for his dignity, warn or control or check him. What she found herself doing was just to treat herself to the middle way. "It was intercepted?"

"It fell into the wrong hands. But there's something in it," he continued to blurt out, "that may be all right. That is, if it's wrong, don't you know? It's all right if it's wrong," he remarkably explained.

What was he, on earth, going to say? Mr. Buckton and the counter-clerk were already interested; no one would have the decency to come in; and she was divided between her particular terror for him and her general curiosity. Yet she already saw with what brilliancy she could add, to carry the thing off, a little false knowledge to all her real. "I quite understand," she said with benevolent, with almost patronising quickness. "The lady has forgotten what she did put."

"Forgotten most wretchedly, and it's an immense inconvenience. It has only just been found that it didn't get there; so that if we could immediately have it—"

"Immediately?"

"Every minute counts. You have," he pleaded, "surely got them on file?"

"So that you can see it on the spot?"

"Yes, please—this very minute." The counter rang with his knuckles, with the knob of his stick, with his panic of alarm. "Do, do hunt it up!" he repeated.

"I dare say we could get it for you," the girl weetly returned.

"Get it?"—he looked aghast. "When?"

"Probably by to-morrow."

"Then it isn't here?"—his face was pitiful.

She caught only the uncovered gleams that peeped out of the blackness, and she wondered what complication, even among the most supposable, the very worst, could be bad enough to account for the degree of his terror. There were twists and turns, there were places where the screw drew blood, that she couldn't guess. She was more and more glad she didn't want to. "It has been sent on."

"But how do you know if you don't look?"

She gave him a smile that was meant to be, in the absolute irony of its propriety, quite divine. "It was August 23rd, and we've nothing later here than August 27th."

Something leaped into his face. "27th—23rd? Then you're sure? You know?"

She felt she scarce knew what—as if she might soon be pounced upon for some lurid connexion with a scandal. It was the queerest of all sensations, for she had heard, she had read, of these things, and the wealth of her intimacy with them at Cocker's might be supposed to have schooled and seasoned her. This particular one that she had really quite lived with was, after all, an old story; yet what it had been before was dim and distant beside the touch under which she now winced. Scandal?—it had never been but a silly word. Now it was a great tense surface, and the surface was somehow Captain Everard's wonderful face. Deep down in his eyes a picture, a scene—a great place like a chamber of justice, where, before a watching crowd, a poor girl, exposed but heroic, swore with a quavering voice to a document, proved an alibi, supplied a link. In this picture she bravely took her place. "It was the 23rd."

"Then can't you get it this morning—or some time to-day?"

She considered, still holding him with her look, which she then turned on her two companions, who were by this time unreservedly enlisted. She didn't care—not a scrap, and she glanced about for a piece of paper. With this she had to recognise the rigour of official thrift—a morsel of blackened blotter was the only loose paper to be seen. "Have you got a card?" she said to her visitor. He was quite away from Paddington now, and the next instant, pocket-book in hand, he had whipped a card out. She gave no glance at the name on it—only turned it to the other side. She continued to hold him, she felt at present, as she had never held him; and her command of her colleagues was for the moment not less marked. She wrote something on the back of the card and pushed it across to him.

He fairly glared at it. "Seven, nine, four—"

"Nine, six, one"—she obligingly completed the number. "Is it right?" she smiled.

He took the whole thing in with a flushed intensity; then there broke out in him a visibility of relief that was simply a tremendous exposure. He shone at them all like a tall lighthouse, embracing even, for sympathy, the blinking young men. "By all the powers—it's wrong!" And without another look, without a word of thanks, without time for anything or anybody, he turned on them the broad back of his great stature, straightened his triumphant shoulders, and strode out of the place.

She was left confronted with her habitual critics. "'If it's wrong it's all right!'" she extravagantly quoted to them.

The counter-clerk was really awe-stricken. "But how did you know, dear?"

"I remembered, love!"

Mr. Buckton, on the contrary, was rude. "And what game is that, miss?"

No happiness she had ever known came within miles of it, and some minutes elapsed before she could recall herself sufficiently to reply that it was none of his business.

CHAPTER XXIV

If life at Cocker's, with the dreadful drop of August, had lost something of its savour, she had not been slow to infer that a heavier blight had fallen on the graceful industry of Mrs. Jordan.

With Lord Rye and Lady Ventnor and Mrs. Bubb all out of town, with the blinds down on all the homes of luxury, this ingenious woman might well have found her wonderful taste left quite on her hands. She bore up, however, in a way that began by exciting much of her young friend's esteem; they perhaps even more frequently met as the wine of life flowed less free from other sources, and each, in the lack of better diversion, carried on with more mystification for the other an intercourse that consisted not a little in peeping out and drawing back. Each waited for the other to commit herself, each profusely curtained for the other the limits of low horizons. Mrs. Jordan was indeed probably the more reckless skirmisher; nothing could exceed her frequent incoherence unless it was indeed her occasional bursts of confidence. Her account of her private affairs rose and fell like a flame in the wind—sometimes the bravest bonfire and sometimes a handful of ashes. This our young woman took to be an effect of the position, at one moment and another, of the famous door of the great world. She had been struck in one of her ha'penny volumes with the translation of a French proverb according to which such a door, any door, had to be either open or shut; and it seemed part of the precariousness of Mrs. Jordan's life that hers mostly managed to be neither. There had been occasions when it appeared to gape wide—fairly to woo her across its threshold; there had been others, of an order distinctly disconcerting, when it was all but banged in her face. On the whole, however, she had evidently not lost heart; these still belonged to the class of things in spite of which she looked well. She intimated that the profits of her trade had swollen so as to float her through any state of the tide, and she had, besides this, a hundred profundities and explanations.

She rose superior, above all, on the happy fact that there were always gentlemen in town and that gentlemen were her greatest admirers; gentlemen from the City in especial—as to whom she was full of information about the passion and pride excited in such breasts by the elements of her charming commerce. The City men did in short go in for flowers. There was a certain type of awfully smart stockbroker—Lord Rye called them Jews and bounders, but she didn't care—whose extravagance, she more than once threw out, had really, if one had any conscience, to be forcibly restrained. It was not perhaps a pure love of beauty: it was a matter of vanity and a sign of business; they wished to crush their rivals, and that was one of their weapons. Mrs. Jordan's shrewdness was extreme; she knew in any case her customer—she dealt, as she said, with all sorts; and it was at the worst a race for her—a race even in the dull months—from one set of chambers to another. And then, after all, there were also still the ladies; the ladies of stockbroking circles were perpetually up and down. They were not quite perhaps Mrs. Bubb or Lady Ventnor; but you couldn't tell the difference unless you quarrelled with them, and then you knew it only by their making-up sooner. These ladies formed the branch of her subject on which she most swayed in the breeze; to that degree that her confidant had ended with an inference or two tending to banish regret for opportunities not embraced. There were indeed tea-gowns that Mrs. Jordan described—but tea-gowns were not the whole of respectability, and it was odd that a clergyman's widow should sometimes speak as if she almost thought so. She came back, it was true, unfailingly to Lord Rye, never, evidently, quite losing sight of him even on the longest excursions. That he was kindness itself had become in fact the very moral it all pointed—pointed in strange flashes of the poor woman's nearsighted eyes. She launched at her young friend portentous looks, solemn heralds of some extraordinary communication. The communication itself, from week to week, hung fire; but it was to the facts over which it hovered that she owed her power of going on. "They are, in one way and another," she often emphasised, "a tower of strength"; and as the allusion was to the aristocracy the girl could quite wonder why, if they were so in "one way," they should require to be so in two. She thoroughly knew, however, how many ways Mrs. Jordan counted in. It all meant simply that her fate was pressing her close. If that fate was to be sealed at the matrimonial altar it was perhaps not remarkable that she shouldn't come all at once to the scratch of overwhelming a mere telegraphist. It would necessarily present to such a person a prospect of regretful sacrifice. Lord Rye—if it was Lord Rye—wouldn't be "kind" to a nonentity of that sort, even though people quite as good had been.

One Sunday afternoon in November they went, by arrangement, to church together; after which—on the inspiration of the moment the arrangement had not included it—they proceeded to Mrs. Jordan's lodging in the region of Maida Vale. She had raved to her friend about her service of predilection; she was excessively "high," and had more than once wished to introduce the girl to the same comfort and privilege. There was a thick brown fog and Maida Vale tasted of acrid smoke; but they had been sitting among chants and incense and wonderful music, during which, though the effect of such things on her mind was great, our young lady had indulged in a series of reflexions but indirectly related to them. One of these was the result of Mrs. Jordan's having said to her on the way, and with a certain fine significance, that Lord Rye had been for some time in town. She had spoken as if it were a circumstance to which little required to be added—as if the bearing of such an item on her life might easily be grasped. Perhaps it was the wonder of whether Lord Rye wished to marry her that made her guest, with thoughts straying to that quarter, quite determine that some other nuptials also should take place at Saint Julian's. Mr. Mudge was still an attendant at his Wesleyan chapel, but this was the least of her worries—it had never even vexed her enough for her to so much as name it to Mrs. Jordan. Mr. Mudge's form of worship was one of several things—they made up in superiority and beauty for what they wanted in number—that she had long ago settled he should take from her, and she had now moreover for the first time definitely established her own. Its principal feature was that it was to be the same as that of Mrs. Jordan and Lord Rye; which was indeed very much what she said to her hostess as they sat together later on. The brown fog was in this hostess's little parlour, where it acted as a postponement of the question of there being, besides, anything else than the teacups and a pewter pot and a very black little fire and a paraffin lamp without a shade. There was at any rate no sign of a flower; it was not for herself Mrs. Jordan gathered sweets. The girl waited till they had had a cup of tea—waited for the announcement that she fairly believed her friend had, this time, possessed herself of her formally at last to make; but nothing came, after the interval, save a little poke at the fire, which was like the clearing of a throat for a speech.

CHAPTER XXV

"I think you must have heard me speak of Mr. Drake?" Mrs. Jordan had never looked so queer, nor her smile so suggestive of a large benevolent bite.

"Mr. Drake? Oh yes; isn't he a friend of Lord Rye?"

"A great and trusted friend. Almost—I may say—a loved friend."

Mrs. Jordan's "almost" had such an oddity that her companion was moved, rather flippantly perhaps, to take it up. "Don't people as good as love their friends when they I trust them?"

It pulled up a little the eulogist of Mr. Drake. "Well, my dear, I love you—"

"But you don't trust me?" the girl unmercifully asked.

Again Mrs. Jordan paused—still she looked queer. "Yes," she replied with a certain austerity; "that's exactly what I'm about to give you rather a remarkable proof of." The sense of its being remarkable was already so strong that, while she bridled a little, this held her auditor in a momentary muteness of submission. "Mr. Drake has rendered his lordship for several years services that his lordship has highly appreciated and that make it all the more—a—unexpected that they should, perhaps a little suddenly, separate."

"Separate?" Our young lady was mystified, but she tried to be interested; and she already saw that she had put the saddle on the wrong horse. She had heard something of Mr. Drake, who was a member of his lordship's circle—the member with whom, apparently, Mrs. Jordan's avocations had most happened to throw her. She was only a little puzzled at the "separation." "Well, at any rate," she smiled, "if they separate as friends—!"

"Oh his lordship takes the greatest interest in Mr. Drake's future. He'll do anything for him; he has in fact just done a great deal. There must, you know, be changes—!"

"No one knows it better than I," the girl said. She wished to draw her interlocutress out. "There will be changes enough for me."

"You're leaving Cocker's?"

The ornament of that establishment waited a moment to answer, and then it was indirect. "Tell me what you're doing."

"Well, what will you think of it?"

"Why that you've found the opening you were always so sure of."

Mrs. Jordan, on this, appeared to muse with embarrassed intensity. "I was always sure, yes—and yet I often wasn't!"

"Well, I hope you're sure now. Sure, I mean, of Mr. Drake."

"Yes, my dear, I think I may say I am. I kept him going till I was."

"Then he's yours?"

"My very own."

"How nice! And awfully rich?" our young woman went on.

Mrs. Jordan showed promptly enough that she loved for higher things. "Awfully handsome—six foot two. And he has put by."

"Quite like Mr. Mudge, then!" that gentleman's friend rather desperately exclaimed.

"Oh not quite!" Mr. Drake's was ambiguous about it, but the name of Mr. Mudge had evidently given her some sort of stimulus. "He'll have more opportunity now, at any rate. He's going to Lady Bradeen."

"To Lady Bradeen?" This was bewilderment. "'Going—'?"

The girl had seen, from the way Mrs. Jordan looked at her, that the effect of the name had been to make her let something out. "Do you know her?"

She floundered, but she found her feet. "Well, you'll remember I've often told you that if you've grand clients I have them too."

"Yes," said Mrs. Jordan; "but the great difference is that you hate yours, whereas I really love mine. Do you know Lady Bradeen?" she pursued.

"Down to the ground! She's always in and out."

Mrs. Jordan's foolish eyes confessed, in fixing themselves on this sketch, to a degree of wonder and even of envy. But she bore up and, with a certain gaiety, "Do you hate her?" she demanded.

Her visitor's reply was prompt. "Dear no!—not nearly so much as some of them. She's too outrageously beautiful."

Mrs. Jordan continued to gaze. "Outrageously?"

"Well, yes; deliciously." What was really delicious was Mrs. Jordan's vagueness. "You don't know her—you've not seen her?" her guest lightly continued.

"No, but I've heard a great deal about her."

"So have I!" our young lady exclaimed.

Jordan looked an instant as if she suspected her good faith, or at least her seriousness. "You know some friend—?"

"Of Lady Bradeen's? Oh yes—I know one."

"Only one?"

The girl laughed out. "Only one—but he's so intimate."

Mrs. Jordan just hesitated. "He's a gentleman?"

"Yes, he's not a lady."

Her interlocutress appeared to muse. "She's immensely surrounded."

"She will be—with Mr. Drake!"

Mrs. Jordan's gaze became strangely fixed. "Is she very good-looking?"

"The handsomest person I know."

Mrs. Jordan continued to brood. "Well, I know some beauties." Then with her odd jerkiness: "Do you think she looks good?"

"Because that's not always the case with the good-looking?"—the other took it up. "No, indeed, it isn't: that's one thing Cocker's has taught me. Still, there are some people who have everything. Lady Bradeen, at any rate, has enough: eyes and a nose and a mouth, a complexion, a figure—"

"A figure?" Mrs. Jordan almost broke in.

"A figure, a head of hair!" The girl made a little conscious motion that seemed to let the hair all down, and her companion watched the wonderful show. "But Mr. Drake is another—?"

"Another?"—Mrs. Jordan's thoughts had to come back from a distance.

"Of her ladyship's admirers. He's 'going,' you say, to her?"

At this Mrs. Jordan really faltered. "She has engaged him."

"Engaged him?"—our young woman was quite at sea.

"In the same capacity as Lord Rye."

"And was Lord Rye engaged?"

CHAPTER XXVI

Mrs. Jordan looked away from her now—looked, she thought, rather injured and, as if trifled with, even a little angry. The mention of Lady Bradeen had frustrated for a while the convergence of our heroine's thoughts; but with this impression of her old friend's combined impatience and diffidence they began again to whirl round her, and continued it till one of them appeared to dart at her, out of the dance, as if with a sharp peck. It came to her with a lively shock, with a positive sting, that Mr. Drake was—could it be possible? With the idea she found herself afresh on the edge of laughter, of a sudden and strange perversity of mirth. Mr. Drake loomed, in a swift image, before her; such a figure as she had seen in open doorways of houses in Cocker's quarter—majestic, middle-aged, erect, flanked on either side by a footman and taking the name of a visitor. Mr. Drake then verily was a person who opened the door! Before she had time, however, to recover from the effect of her evocation, she was offered a vision which quite engulfed it. It was communicated to her somehow that the face with which she had seen it rise prompted Mrs. Jordan to dash, a bit wildly, at something, at anything, that might attenuate criticism. "Lady Bradeen's re-arranging—she's going to be married."

"Married?" The girl echoed it ever so softly, but there it was at last.

"Didn't you know it?"

She summoned all her sturdiness. "No, she hasn't told me."

"And her friends—haven't they?"

"I haven't seen any of them lately. I'm not so fortunate as you."

Mrs. Jordan gathered herself. "Then you haven't even heard of Lord Bradeen's death?"

Her comrade, unable for a moment to speak, gave a slow headshake. "You know it from Mr. Drake?" It was better surely not to learn things at all than to learn them by the butler.

"She tells him everything."

"And he tells you—I see." Our young lady got up; recovering her muff and her gloves she smiled. "Well, I haven't unfortunately any Mr. Drake. I congratulate you with all my heart. Even without your sort of assistance, however, there's a trifle here and there that I do pick up. I gather that if she's to marry any one it must quite necessarily be my friend."

Mrs. Jordan was now also on her feet. "Is Captain Everard your friend?"

The girl considered, drawing on a glove. "I saw, at one time, an immense deal of him."

Mrs. Jordan looked hard at the glove, but she hadn't after all waited for that to be sorry it wasn't cleaner. "What time was that?"

"It must have been the time you were seeing so much of Mr. Drake." She had now fairly taken it in: the distinguished person Mrs. Jordan was to marry would answer bells and put on coals and superintend, at least, the cleaning of boots for the other distinguished person whom she might—well, whom she might have had, if she had wished, so much more to say to. "Good-bye," she added; "good-bye."

Mrs. Jordan, however, again taking her muff from her, turned it over, brushed it off and thoughtfully peeped into it. "Tell me this before you go. You spoke just now of your own changes. Do you mean that Mr. Mudge—?"

"Mr. Mudge has had great patience with me—he has brought me at last to the point. We're to be married next month and have a nice little home. But he's only a grocer, you know"—the girl met her friend's intent eyes—"so that I'm afraid that, with the set you've got into, you won't see your way to keep up our friendship."

Mrs. Jordan for a moment made no answer to this; she only held the muff up to her face, after which she gave it back. "You don't like it. I see, I see."

To her guest's astonishment there were tears now in her eyes. "I don't like what?" the girl asked.

"Why my engagement. Only, with your great cleverness," the poor lady quavered out, "you put it in your own way. I mean that you'll cool off. You already have—!" And on this, the next instant, her tears began to flow. She succumbed to them and collapsed; she sank down again, burying her face and trying to smother her sobs.

Her young friend stood there, still in some rigour, but taken much by surprise even if not yet fully moved to pity. "I don't put anything in any 'way,' and I'm very glad you're suited. Only, you know, you did put to me so splendidly what, even for me, if I had listened to you, it might lead to."

Mrs. Jordan kept up a mild thin weak wail; then, drying her eyes, as feebly considered this reminder. "It has led to my not starving!" she faintly gasped.

Our young lady, at this, dropped into the place beside her, and now, in a rush, the small silly misery was clear. She took her hand as a sign of pitying it, then, after another instant, confirmed this expression with a consoling kiss. They sat there together; they looked out, hand in hand, into the damp dusky shabby little room and into the future, of no such very different suggestion, at last accepted by each. There was no definite utterance, on either side, of Mr. Drake's position in the great world, but the temporary collapse of his prospective bride threw all further necessary light; and what our heroine saw and felt for in the whole business was the vivid reflexion of her own dreams and delusions and her own return to reality. Reality, for the poor things they both were, could only be ugliness and obscurity, could never be the escape, the rise. She pressed her friend—she had tact enough for that—with no other personal question, brought on no need of further revelations, only just continued to hold and comfort her and to acknowledge by stiff little forbearances the common element in their fate. She felt indeed magnanimous in such matters; since if it was very well, for condolence or reassurance, to suppress just then invidious shrinkings, she yet by no means saw herself sitting down, as she might say, to the same table with Mr. Drake. There would luckily, to all appearance, be little question of tables; and the circumstance that, on their peculiar lines, her friend's interests would still attach themselves to Mayfair flung over Chalk Farm the first radiance it had shown. Where was one's pride and one's passion when the real way to judge of one's luck was by making not the wrong but the right comparison? Before she had again gathered herself to go she felt very small and cautious and thankful. "We shall have our own house," she said, "and you must come very soon and let me show it you."

"We shall have our own too," Mrs. Jordan replied; "for, don't you know? he makes it a condition that he sleeps out?"

"A condition?"—the girl felt out of it.

"For any new position. It was on that he parted with Lord Rye. His lordship can't meet it. So Mr. Drake has given him up."

"And all for you?"—our young woman put it as cheerfully as possible.

"For me and Lady Bradeen. Her ladyship's too glad to get him at any price. Lord Rye, out of interest in us, has in fact quite made her take him. So, as I tell you, he will have his own establishment."

Mrs. Jordan, in the elation of it, had begun to revive; but there was nevertheless between them rather a conscious pause—a pause in which neither visitor nor hostess brought out a hope or an invitation. It expressed in the last resort that, in spite of submission and sympathy, they could now after all only look at each other across the social gulf. They remained together as if it would be indeed their last chance, still sitting, though awkwardly, quite close, and feeling also—and this most unmistakeably—that there was one thing more to go into. By the time it came to the surface, moreover, our young friend had recognised the whole of the main truth, from which she even drew again a slight irritation. It was not the main truth perhaps that most signified; but after her momentary effort, her embarrassment and her tears Mrs. Jordan had begun to sound afresh—and even without speaking—the note of a social connexion. She hadn't really let go of it that she was marrying into society. Well, it was a harmless compensation, and it was all the prospective bride of Mr. Mudge had to leave with her.

CHAPTER XXVII

This young lady at last rose again, but she lingered before going. "And has Captain Everard nothing to say to it?"

"To what, dear?"

"Why, to such questions—the domestic arrangements, things in the house."

"How can he, with any authority, when nothing in the house is his?"

"Not his?" The girl wondered, perfectly conscious of the appearance she thus conferred on Mrs. Jordan of knowing, in comparison with herself, so tremendously much about it. Well, there were things she wanted so to get at that she was willing at last, though it hurt her, to pay for them with humiliation. "Why are they not his?"

"Don't you know, dear, that he has nothing?"

"Nothing?" It was hard to see him in such a light, but Mrs. Jordan's power to answer for it had a superiority that began, on the spot, to grow. "Isn't he rich?"

Mrs. Jordan looked immensely, looked both generally and particularly, informed. "It depends upon what you call—! Not at any rate in the least as she is. What does he bring? Think what she has. And then, love, his debts."

"His debts?" His young friend was fairly betrayed into helpless innocence. She could struggle a little, but she had to let herself go; and if she had spoken frankly she would have said: "Do tell me, for I don't know so much about him as that!" As she didn't speak frankly she only said: "His debts are nothing—when she so adores him."

Mrs. Jordan began to fix her again, and now she saw that she must only take it all. That was what it had come to: his having sat with her there on the bench and under the trees in the summer darkness and put his hand on her, making her know what he would have said if permitted; his having returned to her afterwards, repeatedly, with supplicating eyes and a fever in his blood; and her having, on her side, hard and pedantic, helped by some miracle and with her impossible condition, only answered him, yet supplicating back, through the bars of the cage,—all simply that she might hear of him, now for ever lost, only through Mrs. Jordan, who touched him through Mr. Drake, who reached him through Lady Bradeen. "She adores him—but of course that wasn't all there was about it."

The girl met her eyes a minute, then quite surrendered. "What was there else about it?"

"Why, don't you know?"—Mrs. Jordan was almost compassionate.

Her interlocutress had, in the cage, sounded depths, but there was a suggestion here somehow of an abyss quite measureless. "Of course I know she would never let him alone."

"How could she—fancy!—when he had so compromised her?"

The most artless cry they had ever uttered broke, at this, from the younger pair of lips. "Had he so—?"

"Why, don't you know the scandal?"

Our heroine thought, recollected there was something, whatever it was, that she knew after all much more of than Mrs. Jordan. She saw him again as she had seen him come that morning to recover the telegram—she saw him as she had seen him leave the shop. She perched herself a moment on this. "Oh there was nothing public."

"Not exactly public—no. But there was an awful scare and an awful row. It was all on the very point of coming out. Something was lost—something was found."

"Ah yes," the girl replied, smiling as if with the revival of a blurred memory; "something was found."

"It all got about—and there was a point at which Lord Bradeen had to act."

"Had to—yes. But he didn't."

Mrs. Jordan was obliged to admit it. "No, he didn't. And then, luckily for them, he died."

"I didn't know about his death," her companion said.

"It was nine weeks ago, and most sudden. It has given them a prompt chance."

"To get married?"—this was a wonder—"within nine weeks?"

"Oh not immediately, but—in all the circumstances—very quietly and, I assure you, very soon. Every preparation's made. Above all she holds him."

"Oh yes, she holds him!" our young friend threw off. She had this before her again a minute; then she continued: "You mean through his having made her talked about?"

"Yes, but not only that. She has still another pull."

"Another?"

Mrs. Jordan hesitated. "Why, he was in something."

Her comrade wondered. "In what?"

"I don't know. Something bad. As I tell you, something was found."

The girl stared. "Well?"

"It would have been very bad for him. But, she helped him some way—she recovered it, got hold of it. It's even said she stole it!"

Our young woman considered afresh. "Why it was what was found that precisely saved him."

Mrs. Jordan, however, was positive. "I beg your pardon. I happen to know."

Her disciple faltered but an instant. "Do you mean through Mr. Drake? Do they tell him these things?"

"A good servant," said Mrs. Jordan, now thoroughly superior and proportionately sententious, "doesn't need to be told! Her ladyship saved—as a woman so often saves!—the man she loves."

This time our heroine took longer to recover herself, but she found a voice at last. "Ah well—of course I don't know! The great thing was that he got off. They seem then, in a manner," she added, "to have done a great deal for each other."

"Well, it's she that has done most. She has him tight."

"I see, I see. Good-bye." The women had already embraced, and this was not repeated; but Mrs. Jordan went down with her guest to the door of the house. Here again the younger lingered, reverting, though three or four other remarks had on the way passed between them, to Captain Everard and Lady Bradeen. "Did you mean just now that if she hadn't saved him, as you call it, she wouldn't hold him so tight?"

"Well, I dare say." Mrs. Jordan, on the doorstep, smiled with a reflexion that had come to her; she took one of her big bites of the brown gloom. "Men always dislike one when they've done one an injury."

"But what injury had he done her?"

"The one I've mentioned. He must marry her, you know."

"And didn't he want to?"

"Not before."

"Not before she recovered the telegram?"

Mrs. Jordan was pulled up a little. "Was it a telegram?"

The girl hesitated. "I thought you said so. I mean whatever it was."

"Yes, whatever it was, I don't think she saw that."

"So she just nailed him?"

"She just nailed him." The departing friend was now at the bottom of the little flight of steps; the other was at the top, with a certain thickness of fog. "And when am I to think of you in your little home?—next month?" asked the voice from the top.

"At the very latest. And when am I to think of you in yours?"

"Oh even sooner. I feel, after so much talk with you about it, as if I were already there!" Then "Good-bye!" came out of the fog.

"Good-bye!" went into it. Our young lady went into it also, in the opposed quarter, and presently, after a few sightless turns, came out on the Paddington canal. Distinguishing vaguely what the low parapet enclosed she stopped close to it and stood a while very intently, but perhaps still sightlessly, looking down on it. A policeman; while she remained, strolled past her; then, going his way a little further and half lost in the atmosphere, paused and watched her. But she was quite unaware—she was full of her thoughts. They were too numerous to find a place just here, but two of the number may at least be mentioned. One of these was that, decidedly, her little home must be not for next month, but for next week; the other, which came indeed as she resumed her walk and went her way, was that it was strange such a matter should be at last settled for her by Mr. Drake.

At Chalk Farm

A sequel to *In the Cage*
by Henry James

Mary F. Burns

Word by Word
Press

Chalk Farm

Some farmers farm in fruit, some farm in grain,
Others farm in dairy stuff, and many farm in vain,
But I know a place for a Sunday morning's walk
Where the Farmer and his Family only farm in chalk.
The Farmer and his Family before you walk back
Will bid you in to sit awhile and share
their mid-day snack –
O they that live in Chalk Farm they live at their ease,
For the Farmer and his Family can't tell
chalk from cheese.

—Eleanor Farjean in her 1916 book
Nursery Rhymes of London Town.

At Chalk Farm

One

As before, it had occurred to her early in her newly attained position—that of a young wife finding herself in a house of her own, with a husband going off to work six and a half days each week—that her possibilities of knowing many persons outside her new confinement might be enhanced if she could find certain opportunities that would overcome, or obviate, the many obstacles she had already encountered. But the source of those opportunities remained as yet obscure. She had steadily declined to hear her husband's hints as to the pecuniary advantage to them of her taking up her former work as a telegraphist within the—it must be admitted, superior—surroundings of his grocery establishment in the London suburb of Chalk Farm, despite the hams, cheeses, laundry soap and tinned beef arrayed outside the telegraph cage. There, unlike her previous labor at Cocker's smaller, smellier, darker and dimmer store, her husband's new venture offered light and air, spaciousness and cleanliness. He had, she knew within herself, a certain genius for the business, and the constantly increasing numbers of well-heeled customers attested to that fact.

There would, she also knew, be, therefore, vastly enlarged opportunities for her powers of curiosity and observation, her former, at least, delight and satisfaction in encountering, remembering, cataloging and yes, judging,

At Chalk Farm

the vices and (less often) virtues of said well-heeled personages as they paraded them before her in the countless words (except that it was her job to count them) written into telegrams they sent across the city and over to the continent, sometimes several times a day —arrangements, assignations, reservations, coded love notes, warnings and, occasionally, downright tedious nonsense. Nonetheless, she felt it, somehow, due to her sensibilities and her removal (at last) from the human disagreeablenesses of Mayfair, to allow herself—for a space of time at least—a freer range of view, of movement, even of thought contemplating a larger landscape than the mere inside of a shop, however clean.

She was, in short, content to be in the house for now, in her *home* as she wonderingly termed it to herself, and spend her time arraying—as a spread of Tarot cards on the table—the possibilities of encounters she might experience when she was ready to step outside. She had read, in the newspapers, of the influx of women to the work world more and more—as clerks in fashionable stores, as typists for eminent men of letters, as librarians in the great and small libraries planted throughout the metropolis—though she admitted to herself that her own narrow range of reading material might not qualify her for such an exalted post—and, as an old friend had done, in the creation of a position of genteel service that answered a need the wealthy had hitherto not known they had: in this case, the managing and arrangement of flowers for their highly sociable drawing and dining rooms. So she sat, in the house, musing upon her possibilities and choices, unwilling to move outside its close environs and yet, longing to do so.

At Chalk Farm

Two

The house in Chalk Farm, which was set as close to the grander crescents of large and airy homes as such a small house could be, was positioned so as to turn its back, so to speak, on the East, where were the low-roofed scrums of poorer folk who had only gotten so far as this edge of Camden Town on their way to make their fortunes in the city, after lingering too long on the dreary farms to the north. Our young wife—she had not yet become adjusted to the name she had but two months prior taken on as her own, therefore we will refrain from calling her by her new name until she herself admits her readiness to acknowledge it and hear it applied to herself—knew that Chalk Farm was a mere three and a half miles from the steps of St. Paul's, but it might as well have been a hundred. The house itself was well-built and solid, rather like Mr Mudge (her husband) himself, of a variety of muddy-colored stone and brick, and wooden casements with shutters painted brown, much as his clear eyes were framed by dark brows above and a high rise of only slightly less dark beard on his cheeks.

One approached the house via a foreshortened brick walk from the street to the doorstep with two patches of dirt to either side that might become flowers or grass in the spring—it being the dead of winter now, a January of sleet and rain and lowering grey skies—and beyond the door, a foursquare structure of rooms, with an attic above and a root cellar below, and a minimal niche set into an added-on sort of lean-to near the kitchen in the back, into which our young woman's shadowy presence of a mother had been installed.

Our former telegraphist had rarely been at leisure in all her life for more than an afternoon—not since the onset of her family's misery in her early years, after her father died

At Chalk Farm

of despair and her young brother of fever, leaving her, her sister and her mother in the unspeakable position of genteel females without any male support. Her sister, older than she by some ten years, who had for a while contributed her meagre earnings from sewing and dress-making to keep their souls within their bodies, had announced one day she was moving to York to live with two other women of her acquaintance, where they had applied for work in a cotton mill and been accepted. After a postcard that was merely informative of her having arrived safely in the North, they had never heard from her again. Our young woman had promptly gone out to procure steady work of her own, and had lighted, with great good luck, on the telegraphist's position at the grocery store wherein worked the estimable Mr Mudge, her then future husband.

Now, as she sat in the tiny "front room," wrapped in two lengths of a shawl, her feet nearly touching the rim of the stove in which a low coal fire muttered, she contemplated with no little wonder how she had come to this juncture in her life, and where she would go from here. She had, of necessity, to 'do' for themselves in their quiet domestic domain—cooking, cleaning, buying, washing—but to that she was inured as well as efficient, from long practice. Her mother was equally as long incapable of providing any assistance with household chores; prior to their removal to the little home in Chalk Farm, her mother's days were misted over by a too frequent application of gin or whiskey, when it could be afforded. Here, now, although Mr Mudge's larger providence could make for something close to enough, nonetheless this particular medication was thriftily doled out, in actual thimblefuls, to calm the old lady's jittery nerves and, frankly, keep her somnolent and mostly comfortable. Our young woman didn't begrudge her

At Chalk Farm

mother that comfort, nor her husband his occasional pint, but she herself had never felt the interest or need to indulge in anything that dulled the cares and troubles of her quotidian existence—her imagination, deep and broad, was her chosen exhilaration, the elixir that helped shine a warm, romantic light on her fellow creatures and their ever-varying circumstances.

Three

She exercised it now, her imagination, as she sat by the stove in the interim of rest that followed after making and serving luncheon to her mother, and before the labor of dinner and other duties were to be taken up. Frankly, she thought with some irritation, how on earth Mr Mudge could entertain the notion that she return to work every day was beyond her comprehension. She and her mother had managed together, as to laundry, food and such, with the help of a neighbor as well as a basic indifference (especially on her mother's part) to finery of costume, or comfortable surroundings in their mean boarding house quarters; at work, our young woman required only neatness and modesty of dress. Mr Mudge, on the other hand, as a bachelor, had taken his evening meals at home, thriftily, on an abundance of leavings and titbits from the grocery store produce and meat counters; his luncheons were provided at the shop. When he became a partner in the new grocery, in a managing position, before they married, his aprons and shirts were supplied by the establishment, and sent out regularly for cleaning and pressing. And as she grudgingly conceded, these perquisites were still in force—but nonetheless, there were household linens, towels, napkins, in addition to her

At Chalk Farm

own and her mother's clothing, that required attention and laundering. Who would do all that if she were to leave the house every day for work outside?

She thought that his desire to have her in the shop with him was simply that—he wanted to be with her all day, not in any way to observe or control or master her—she had made sure at the first that he was not that sort of man—but again, simply, because he wanted to *be with her*. She puffed out a short sigh of annoyance tempered by affection. She had wondered, before her marriage, how married people managed it—the being in each other's company for days on end, to say nothing of the nights—to see the same face at the start of every day and at the close of every evening. Granted, after a week or so of awkward and unfamiliar closeness in the reaches of the night—they had begun with a brief honeymoon of three days at a hotel in Brighton—she had become accustomed to his large, warm presence in the bed, and almost—*almost*—imagined that she might miss him if he were not there.

As during their courtship of nearly a year, she felt superior to him, as she did to most people, but there were times when he would surprise her, amuse her, endear himself to her by coming out with some observation or magnanimity or understanding that showed him to have depths beyond her initial ken of him. She settled again within herself that she had made the right decision, coming to Chalk Farm and all that it brought to her—and all that she had left behind, unchosen, pushed away, in fact—denied.

Her thoughts went instantly to Captain Everard, and Lady Bradeen, and the scandal that she herself had felt lap about her very boot tips last autumn, when things had come to a crisis, there in the claustrophobic wire telegraphy cage at Cocker's grocery and post office. Mr Mudge had already,

At Chalk Farm

some months before, left his place there to climb to higher heights and cleaner air than Mayfair, though not nearly, in her estimation, air so imbued with daring and excitement, with—should she say it?—the luscious sin of ha'penny-novel emotions run amok. Where were they, the two of them, right now, this very minute? At some European watering place? Or, more likely, as it was the Winter Season, at Lady Bradeen's grand house in Mayfair. Ever since her ladyship's husband had become the late, lamented (or not) Lord Bradeen, she'd had a free hand with her pampered life, to live as she saw fit—and to live it with Captain Everard, as he saw fit to do as well.

Our young woman knew there was one person who could bring her up-to-date on the whole affair, but she had so far, in the past three or four months, denied herself the reaching out to that former friend, from a sense of compassion as well as a determined dislike of appearing to harbor a low curiosity about the details of the daily lives of former adulterers.

Four

A short time later that same afternoon, as if conjured by her musing, and because she could see, facing the window as she was, a figure walk up the miniscule brick walkway—she perceived that Mrs Jordan herself was about to knock on her door. Nay, Mrs Drake now! There was no servant to answer the knock—and our young housewife almost laughed to think that answering her own door was all too like the butler whom this old friend of hers had unaccountably married. But Mrs Jordan—*Mrs Drake*—was a fellow traveller from older, harder times, when she, a clergyman's widow, had joined with our heroine's own family to share the precious apples and occasional orange or spare potato they bestowed upon each other, to supplement the boarding house fare. She was, in any event, an equal in quality, and, not unlike like our young woman, had found in herself an enterprising spirit that lifted her above her poverty while maintaining a genteel appearance—Mrs Drake was the old friend who "did" flowers for the well-born ladies and well-dressed gentlemen bachelors in London—dressing their dining tables and drawing rooms with blooms and greens, palms and orchids and tulips by the dozens, by the hundreds—a vocation she had created on her own, and which had served her well enough to meet and then marry a proper, abstemious and deserving butler in the home of one of her bachelor clients. They had since then removed to a small flat of their own, while Mr Drake took on new duties at the home of Lady Bradeen, who had enticed him away from her friend's establishment.

"Mrs Drake!" Our young wife smiled and greeted her visitor as if with surprise. "How wonderful to see you here at last!" She held the door open wide, and bid her friend enter.

"You will, I know, forgive me for not giving you notice of my coming," Mrs Drake said in a hurried but unconcerned manner, while taking time to look about the scant four feet of entrance way inside the door. There was little enough to see—a rag rug on the wooden floor, an umbrella stand, and a small, old wooden table—perhaps to hold the post—under a slightly time-spotted oval mirror which hung on the painted, not papered, wall above it.

Mrs Drake smiled as she handed over her coat and umbrella and gloves, and, as the two women's eyes met and

At Chalk Farm

stayed for a moment longer, her smile deepened and broadened; her eyes misted slightly, as did our own young woman's, and the two friends embraced, irresistibly, holding each other with soft murmurs into which volumes of past misery, shared poverty, and the consciousness of their grateful, more comfortable lives in the present were compressed. They stepped back after a brief minute, each reverting somewhat to the more presentable, distanced face and form that their emotional exchange had momentarily effaced.

"I'm so pleased to see you," said our young wife, and she felt as if she truly meant it. "Are you able to stay for some tea?"

"And I you," said Mrs Drake, and nodded her acquiescence to refreshment. The cold air of the wintry outdoors had burst into the small house with her, but the door was soon firmly closed, and the visitor was shown into the front room with every courtesy. The lady of the house quickly assembled tea and biscuits and carried them into the front room on a tray that had been the wedding gift of the very person to whom she was serving the repast—a fine, black lacquered tray painted with Japanese-style pink peonies and tendrils of green leaves sedately riotous in the center. Mrs Drake acknowledged the use of her gift with a slight lift of her eyebrows and a small, pleased smile.

They poured and drank their tea a few moments in silence, neither one seemingly inclined to break the silence that grew between them. The unspoken question that the one was dying to ask, and the other equally fervent in wishing to answer, hung therefore in the room with its own unsettling presence.

With a delicate flourish, Mrs Drake lowered her cup to the saucer, placed it on the table between them, and leaned

At Chalk Farm

forward to speak, her eagerness at last overcoming her sense of decorum.

"My dear," she whispered, "they have set a date!"

"What!" cried our young lady, startled out of her desire to remain composed. "So soon! Surely it is not announced."

Mrs Drake shook her head, demurring. "It is only spoken of among their intimates as what may—or will—happen at some time, but I have been honored with more specifics." She arched an eyebrow knowingly, filled with a satisfaction that seemed to relay she could know no greater happiness than in being thus confided in by her Ladyship. "It is to be a relatively quiet affair, of course, and will take place in the country, early in the Spring, only six months after…." Her voice drifted off. *After His Lordship's death*, our young woman supplied silently.

Mrs Drake spoke again. "It is all to be kept quite among the family for the time being. But even a small wedding at the Bradeen's country estate, however, as you must imagine, will not be without its grandeur and glamour, and will of course be much talked of."

"But even there—or perhaps, especially there, in the country, even with so few people attending," our young woman pursued, smiling a little, "there will be need of flowers for the wedding, and the reception, and the dinners and breakfasts before and after, will there not?"

"You have it quite right," Mrs Drake said, triumphantly. "We have talked of it all, myself and her Ladyship, many times. She has quite a sense for color, but nothing of arrangement." She brought herself up proudly. "She leaves it all in my hands."

At Chalk Farm

There still hovered in the air above their heads the more pointed, and poignant, question that our young woman wished more than ever to hear the answer to.

"And Captain Everard?" she said, looking for all the world as if it were an indifferent question, to whose answer she was herself indifferent. "How does he regard these proceedings?"

"Oh! My dear," said Mrs Drake, laughing a little. Her glance at her tea cup reminded our young hostess of her duties, and she poured more tea and offered more biscuits as Mrs Drake continued. "He is greatly amused, he says, at all the fuss and bother, but wishes to be indulgent to her Ladyship." She paused a moment for a bite of biscuit—one of the better sort to be found at Mr Mudge's establishment, and a great favorite with the ladies, a lemon-scented, buttery confection in the shape of a half seashell. Mrs Drake looked thoughtful. "I'm not sure, however, but that he wouldn't prefer something infinitely less arranged, less grand, less…parading." She immediately looked stricken at having caught herself out in a momentary lapse of loyalty to Lady Bradeen. "That is," she began correcting herself, "not quite what I meant, of course. Her Ladyship has excellent taste in everything."

"I believe I understand," said our young woman, nodding thoughtfully. She could discern in Mrs Drake's slip of the tongue exactly—so she thought—what Captain Everard was objecting to about his forthcoming nuptials. His was not a showy nor a reflective nature—both his military training and his education fitted him more for restraint and reticence than defying society's expectations with bluster or glamour—but then, he had, after all, thought our young woman, broken through that restraint when he took up with

At Chalk Farm

Lady Bradeen in the first place. His air of amused optimism, his seeming wonder at everyday events, his thorough good nature and affable way, came back to her with a force. She shook her head without knowing she did it, perplexed again at the power of such a great passion that it would so disrupt the very nature and pattern of being of such a man as to make him act in ways, if not contradictory, then at least countering to, his desire to be a mild and accommodating presence in the world.

"Why do you shake your head?" asked her visitor, leaning forward again with some concern.

Our young woman made herself reply easily, brushing off the slight unease. "Nothing! I only see him—as I so often did see him"—(she couldn't resist emphasizing her superior—*then*—knowledge of and acquaintance with the Captain)—"with that endearing hesitation, that affable politeness that covered over a heart wishing only quiet comfort and happy times."

"He does not have a flair for society, as Lady Bradeen has," Mrs Drake said solemnly, "but then, one does not expect that so much of a man, and a soldier at that, unless of course, he is one of the bachelors."

Both women nodded in agreement. Our young woman decided that was enough talk about Captain Everard.

"So will you then, be off soon to the country, to…Lindisfarne, isn't it? The Bradeen's estate?" Our young woman smiled to herself at Mrs Drake's surprised look, which was quickly replaced by a smile of that lady's own.

"You are very sharp, I see," she said to her young friend. "Yes, I will be going there in the advance guard, as it were, and Mr Drake, of course, will follow to manage the household as he does so well," she added with demure

At Chalk Farm

pride. She was suddenly serious, and leaned forward to lay her hand on her friend's.

"And that is what I have particularly come today to speak with you about," she said. "I know we spoke of this once before—you taking up with me and my *benefices* to my clients, as it were, my floral ministrations—but I need someone to help now, more desperately than ever—I need you, my dear! I know you would bring good sense, taste and gentility to the task, and not let me down."

Our young woman drew back her hand in consternation, equally surprised at Mrs Drake's proposal as she was conscious of her own heart beating insistently fast. When she could speak, she merely said, "Please explain to me what all this would entail, dear Mrs Drake."

Five

She found she couldn't help but feel somewhat nervous, later that evening, despite her knowing that her husband—solid, unreflecting grocery man that he was—was unlikely to object to nearly any proposition she might put forward—he who had shown not the slightest jealousy or mistrust when she had, last summer, put it to him that she wanted to stay on at Cocker's, and thus delay their wedding day, in order to "help" Captain Everard, in order to keep her promise to the Captain, made one extraordinary afternoon when the two of them had chanced to meet in a park and have an extraordinary conversation, her promise to "do anything, do everything" for him. Additionally, her husband, she knew, would not object to a scheme that would bring a monetary increase to their newly formed household. Nonetheless, and perhaps it was only the *frisson* of excitement, the anticipation of possibly one day entering Lady Bradeen's house—she was a trifle nervous.

"I have something to tell you," she said, choosing the opportune moment after she had escorted her aged mother back to her niche next to the dreary kitchen, and before her husband took up the evening newspaper—he was, though a grocer, a man who liked to be informed. Mr Mudge, all mildness and attention, looked up at her from his chair by the stove. Her fingers knitted themselves against the back of the overstuffed twin to his seat, behind which she stood.

"I have engaged myself," she began—and suddenly wondered if she should phrase it more as a question than a statement, but of course now it was too late—"to become a junior partner with Mrs Drake—Mrs Jordan that was, you remember—in her floral arrangement business."

Mr Mudge laid down the paper he had taken up before she had begun. He leaned back in his chair, and she saw a gleam of interest in his eyes.

"Do you know enough about flowers and their arrangement?" he asked, with no little keenness, she thought, "to undertake such tasks for Mrs Drake's city clients?"

She answered easily. "Mrs Drake thinks so."

"And," he swiftly followed up, "she wouldn't be likely to injure her own interests." He nodded, thinking it over. "You say, 'junior partner'—does this require any capital input?"

She shook her head, then enlarged upon the negative. "Not in the way of funds, that is," she said. "Naturally, I will be obliged to purchase some rather more suitable clothing." She was relieved when he merely nodded again.

"And the pay?"

At Chalk Farm

This question irritated her, as placing too much interest in the pecuniary, instead of the imagined glories and opportunities the situation offered her. But she knew it was important, too.

"I am offered a third of the fee for any services Mrs Drake and I work on together—there may be some she can do herself, others that will require my assistance—it will not be, and I approve of this, a full-time, daily prospect. If I were to do a situation on my own, the entire fee would be mine."

His next question surprised her more, perhaps, than anything he had ever said to her in their life together. "And will you go to Lady Bradeen's?" he asked, not at all with any increase of interest, or alarm, or judgement. "And is Captain Everard still hanging about?"

She eyed him with a severe look that belied both her amusement and her wonder at this odd man she had married. Her approval of his lack of concern, his lack of simple spousal jealousy and possessiveness, was somewhat at war with her romantic notions of passion and drama. But she was, our young wife, preeminently practical and, truth be told, wise to the ways of the world she inhabited. She knew, it shall be said, upon which side her bread was buttered, and she liked it that way.

"I believe he is," she said, with a slow, almost conspiratorial smile at her Mr Mudge. "It will be interesting to me to see him, to see them, in their connubial habitat."

"They are married—already?" Mr Mudge echoed her own astonishment from earlier in the day, and she quickly shook her head.

- 151 -

"Soon, soon," she said. "And it's all to be kept quiet, probably only a mere few dozens of guests at Lindisfarne"—she savored the name on her tongue—"in a few months' time."

"Not in town, then," he said. And looked at her again, thoughtfully. "And will you be obliged to be at this Lindisfarne yourself, to look after the arranging of the connubial flowers?"

"Yes," she said. "In company with Mrs Drake, of course, and for that matter, of Mr Drake."

He nodded, appearing to appreciate the situation as she presented it.

"You are satisfied, then," he continued, and seemed prepared to take up his newspaper again, "that you will like this floral work and find the terms acceptable?"

She nodded, her hands loosing their grip on the large chair.

"Good, then," he said, turning to his paper after smiling up at her. "Good."

Six

She stood in the larger drawing room of Lady Bradeen's grand house in Mayfair, partially concealed behind an enormous Chinese vase on a low, carved wooden pedestal, framed by dark green velvet draperies which hung floor to ceiling in the high, dim room. Mrs Drake had left her an hour ago, to see about some flowers that had not arrived—she wanted to berate the florist in person. Lady Bradeen's dinner party tonight—twenty people, some of them truly august personages—must be given special attention, and Mrs Drake had required our young woman to attend her for

At Chalk Farm

this, her first significant experience in helping with a very grand arrangement—and her first venture into Lady Bradeen's house. There had been many other flowery ministrations in the time since Mrs Drake had visited Chalk Farm with her offer of partnership—in the apartments of the bachelor clients, even a private dinner at a French restaurant in Bloomsbury, where our young woman's odd imagination had struck upon the precise kinds of flowers and greenery that the Bohemian-affected young ladies and gentleman found acceptably anti-bourgeois and appropriately poetic. Mrs Drake had been excessively pleased with her.

She plucked away at a chrysanthemum that didn't know its place, and as she leaned into the fragrance of its perfume, she heard someone enter the room. She froze, her hand raised to the wayward blossom.

Captain Everard—for it was he, as her heart had forewarned her so that she would keep still—slowly walked across the room to the French doors that were open to the back garden—it was a warm afternoon, but still early Spring, with the sun hidden behind a sheen of grey clouds that hung low, threatening rain.

She watched, trying not to breathe. It was the first time she had seen him since last autumn—and she observed him carefully. He was quiet, not just in his movements, but in his very being—there was a stillness, a lack—she could only think of it in the negative—a lack of energy, of life, even of motion. He was listless. He drooped. This was not the man to whom she had declared, all those months ago, that she would do anything for him—*everything* for him—when the threat of scandal was heavy above his head, and she had held the key that would ward off disgrace.

At Chalk Farm

What she had helped him obtain had not, after all, answered. He was not happy, and she felt as if, somehow, she had failed him.

Oh, why had she come to this house? She should not have come. What good would it do her—or him—for him to know she saw his unhappiness? To see face to face his failure, which was also somehow hers?

What had she to do with him now?

A sudden cramp in her leg, from the effort of standing absolutely still, caused her to shift her position and in doing so, she jostled the table, which made a small scraping sound on the floor. Captain Everard immediately turned in her direction.

"Who's that?" he said. "Is someone there?"

Our young woman did the simplest thing she could do—she stepped forward from behind the flowers, and nodded her head in a brief curtsey to the Captain. "I'm sorry, sir," she said, reasonably well composed. "I didn't mean to startle you—you came in so quietly I just now knew you were here."

The Captain, for his part, was staring at her, pulling his fair, full mustache with one hand, as he stood before the tall windows, the other hand lodged behind his back, the light coming from behind him obscuring whatever look might be on his face. She stepped forward a little, somewhat sideways to him, hoping that would make him move out of the doorframe and therefore allow more light on his face. Her tactic was successful, and she was gratified to see the light of recognition break in his handsome face, accompanied by a smile and a cordial gleam in his eye.

"It's you!" he said, again emanating that almost childlike, ingenuous wonder at common events that she had

At Chalk Farm

found so amusing in him. "Why, goodness me, whatever are you doing here?"

She smiled at this, and didn't respond immediately, which gave him just the time he needed to realize how atrociously unmannerly such a question was. Every emotion played freely and largely across his face, and she read it all, quickly, deeply, with great delight and no little emotion of her own. She felt glad, more than she knew she should, that upon this, their second-ever meeting (outside the telegraph cage, that is), she was better dressed than before, looked less like a girl who worked at such a place as Cocker's and more like a young lady who mixed, as one might say, with the right sort of people. Mrs Drake had commended her new way of styling her hair that morning, allowing the rich brown gleam of it a fair play against her cheeks before gathering it in a loose chignon at the back. She felt, at last, that she could almost be said to be pretty—as her friend had often told her she was.

"Excuse me, that is, I didn't mean," Captain Everard stumbled his way back to politeness, then stopped talking altogether. He took a step closer, his smile widening. "It is you, isn't it? The girl from the telegraph office?"

Our young woman, still smiling, though not so broadly as the Captain, spoke at last. "Yes, it is I, the 'girl' from the telegraph office."

"I say!" said the Captain, pulling harder at his mustache, then running a quick hand through his fair mop of hair. "I say!" he said again.

"I'm here, with Mrs Drake, to do the flowers for the dinner party this evening," said our heroine, gesturing slightly toward the bower of chrysanthemums behind which she had hidden.

At Chalk Farm

"Ah, well," said Captain Everard, nodding his head. "Of course, yes, flowers...and all that. I say," he burst out again, "you know, I don't even know your name."

Our young woman looked down, as if a bit bashful, and moved another step closer to him. "I have changed my name since we last spoke." She looked at him a little sideways, pretending to look out at the garden. She could feel a few tender rays of sunshine as they fell upon her shoulders and arms, a lovely effect on the dark green bombazine of her dress.

"You have married," he said, solemnly and with a slow kind of thoughtfulness, even a wonder. They exchanged long glances here, and the former telegraphist nearly blushed at the implications of him being cognizant of the kind of experience she now had, which she hadn't had before.

"It does happen," our young woman said after a moment, with a hint of amusement. "Many women are trying out the state these days, I understand. Men as well."

A flush of red across the Captain's cheeks made her think he rather sensitively took that statement to heart. She hastened to cover his embarrassment.

"My married name is Mudge," she announced, mindful on the instant that—strangest of strange coincidences—one of the nicknames the Captain's friends used for him in their various telegraphic communications was "Mudge," and she watched him narrowly.

"You don't say!" he said, apparently delighted. "You know, some of my friends call me that! Why, I never!" He took a step back and bowed a courtier's bow before her, one arm thrown back and the other across his front. "*Bien venue*, Mrs Mudge! Welcome to this house."

At Chalk Farm

As he straightened up from his bow, she saw a sudden look of consternation take hold of his eyes, and he stood as if struck by a fearful thought.

"Does she, your Mrs Drake—Lady Bradeen's Mrs Drake, I guess—does she know our ... connection?" He looked at her with round eyes, holding his breath.

The poor dear, thought our Mrs Mudge—for as she has announced and acknowledged the name, so shall we—he has just now thought of the possibilities, the drama, the reminder of their beginnings, that my presence in this house can mean. But she didn't have the heart to toy with him.

"No," she said simply. "Unless you have informed Lady Bradeen? And I do believe she is highly unlikely to recognize me in any event, she consults only with Mrs Drake, and I am but a hired hand to her—only we two together know the particulars of all that passed last autumn."

They stood closer than ever in the afternoon light from the French doors, about two feet apart, and there seemed too much in the air between them to give it any kind of life in words. Their silence grew until it became something they could almost touch with outstretched fingers.

The door to the drawing room opened and Mrs Drake's soft tones could be heard as she was ushered through the door by the butler—in point of fact, by her husband, Mr Drake—and came to a stop as she beheld her junior partner and Captain Everard standing together.

"Ah, Captain," she called out gaily, instantly covering her initial start of surprise. "You have met my junior partner, Mrs Mudge!"

At Chalk Farm

Seven

It had been a subject of much and repeated discussion between Mrs Drake and Mrs Mudge—the manner in which they must behave when the inevitable, so it seemed to them, meeting of Captain Everard and his former telegraphist should occur. They had agreed that Lady Bradeen would not recognize the young woman, having seen her only twice or three times, and that was almost a year ago, and through the bars and smudged window of the telegraphist's cage in Mr Cocker's store. Mrs Mudge smiled to herself then, remembering the various pseudonyms her Ladyship had used for her telegraphic communications—Cissy the one most often used, but sometimes Mary—but so did they all, those ladies who seemed to our young woman to be ever so much more in pursuit of the gentlemen than the other way around. But Cissy, or Mary, or her Ladyship, had been the most beautiful of the beautiful, with her magnificent manners and the unconscious haughtiness that told of her birth, her father and mother, her cousins, and all her ancestors in nothing more nor less than the lift of a finger as she wrote out the words of a telegram.

They had also agreed, with many an arched brow and knowing look on Mrs Drake's part, that she, Mrs Drake, should never admit to the slightest bit of information regarding the role her junior partner may have played in the drama of the previous summer and autumn, or that she herself had knowledge of any part of it beyond what could be imagined she already knew, given her marriage to Mr Drake. She would be the consummate actress, she assured her young friend, and the Captain would, by all their efforts and at all costs, be made to feel comfortable that his former acquaintance might occasionally be present in his lady's home, and no one the wiser.

Mrs Mudge congratulated herself privately on never having revealed half the information about the Captain and her Ladyship that she had learned during that time, and magnanimously allowed Mrs Drake to think that she—Mrs Drake—knew more of the actual details of the scandal than did Mrs Mudge. The previous November, before either of our two ladies had entered the matrimonial state, Mrs Drake (then Mrs Jordan) had been the one to inform her young friend that Lady Bradeen had been the savior of the drama, that she—Lady Bradeen—had "found" whatever had been "lost" and by doing so, had rescued the Captain from the consequences of something he had done, something "very bad", so bad it was not to be named. And furthermore, she had added in a whisper, though it was only the two of them in Mrs Drake's room, the Captain was poor as a church mouse, and in debt up to his ears—all of which, upon the sudden and timely (for the two lovers) death of Lord Bradeen, her Ladyship had, in a word, fixed. Our Mrs Mudge did not give any credulity to such a tale, and thought—with contempt for her Ladyship, and pity for the Captain—that such histrionics boded ill for their marriage.

Eight

The time was fast approaching when Mrs Drake and her junior partner were to travel out to Lindisfarne, an estate to the north and west of London, to reconnoiter and begin to plan for the great and solemn nuptial event and all its attendant lunches, suppers, dinners and receptions.

At Chalk Farm

Mrs Mudge was to learn, courtesy of Mrs Drake's gracious confidences, that her Ladyship had been greatly enlarging her original "small, quiet" plan into something rather more grand and magnificent. When Lady Bradeen had married, at seventeen, a widower three times her age, it was deemed a fitting match as to family, society, and fortune on both sides—but it seemed that now, at twenty-five, she viewed her current march to the altar as her 'real' marriage, and therefore, her 'real' wedding, despite the small fortune her parents had laid out for the ceremony with Lord Bradeen. In consequence, the guest list had swelled from twenty to fifty, and the duration of the festivities at Lindisfarne grew from three days to a full week.

Mrs Drake was in a rational flurry as to where flowers of any sort, to say nothing of the best sort, could be found in sufficient numbers in the middle of April. She instructed her junior partner, with an anxious smile, to pray for an early Spring.

The day of their journey to the country estate of the Bradeen family came, a fair and windy Saturday, and Mrs Mudge found herself anxious and perplexed at her feelings upon so leaving her husband and her mother to shift for themselves. She had adopted the expedient of asking a friend of her mother's from their boarding house days, a woman fit and amiable and able, to come to the house at Chalk Farm for the eight or so days that she, Mrs Mudge, would be absent. Clara Brown, this amiable helper, had been by earlier in the week to receive instructions and was as reassuring as she could be as to all matters of food, laundry, groceries, house cleaning, and keeping an eye on mother. She had readily accepted the better-than-modest stipend offered for such tasks and service—our Mrs Mudge felt she could easily spare the amount from the seemingly

At Chalk Farm

enormous fee she and Mrs Drake would be sharing. It put her in mind of the way she had marvelled at the endless shillings and pounds—daily!—that "her" gentlemen and ladies in the former days at Cocker's would lay down at her window, merely to send a message to a friend that a party had been delightful, or that the new cravats at Brown's were such as one had never before seen. One day's worth of the money spent on telegrams would have fed her mother, her sister (when she was present) and herself for months on end! She had wondered then, enviously, resentfully, how she might—*if* she might *ever*—partake of the shower of gold that fell continuously before her eyes—and now, perhaps, a small sprinkle of that munificence seemed to be coming to her.

Mr Mudge, in his solemn and business-like way, had expressed his feelings on the occasion.

"Well, I won't half like you being gone so long, my dear," he said, kissing her on the forehead, the morning of her leaving, before he left for the grocery shop. He had looked at her kindly, and a strange emotion played across his face. "If you should need me at any point, you can send a message straight to the shop."

His wife had looked up at him with some surprise. "What on earth should I need you for, out there in the country?" She colored at the rude sound of that, and tried to amend it with a joke. "Well, we certainly will call on you if we run out of ham or biscuits!"

He continued to look a little strange, then taking her in his large arms and holding her to him, so she could smell the strong orange soap he used on his neck and face, he murmured to her, "All the same, remember you have a man who will protect you."

At Chalk Farm

She was strangely moved by his statement, and wondered if there was some danger or discomfort that he intuited in her situation to which she herself was blind. In his promise of protection, she was reminded of an incident that took place in Cocker's, before they had begun walking out, when a drunken and violent man had burst into the place and began wildly to grab at customers' belongings and purses, seizing money from hands outstretched across the counters. She, in her cage, along with the two young men who worked there with her, had frozen, aghast at the tumult—indeed, the two young men, she recalled later, had recoiled and nearly hid themselves in the back of the cage. But Mr Mudge had calmly and quickly grasped the situation, strode out from behind the counter and, grabbing the man by his collar, had shown him the door and the cobblestones outside in no uncertain terms. From inside the shop, they could hear shouting and scuffles and, a moment later, the shrill whistle of a policeman on the beat. A few minutes later, Mr Mudge had come back inside, his white apron only a slight bit dirtied from his tussle with the miscreant, but his dark hair unmussed and his countenance serene. The whole place had burst into applause, which Mr Mudge acknowledged with a slight nod of his head and only a very faint blush upon his robust cheeks. She always thought that it was what had done the trick in turning her thoughts to him as a future husband.

As she closed the door to the house and turned back to manage her own leave-taking, she shook her head at the idea of needing protection at Lindisfarne—but she felt comforted all the same.

At Chalk Farm

Nine

Unlike Mrs Drake, who, with her late husband the vicar, had made up a humble couple invited to Sunday teas and the occasional small dinner party at the country estate under whose patronage her husband's vicarage duties had been performed—unlike her, our Mrs Mudge was not familiar with the vastnesses and lengths and breadths, the high ceilings and the acres of books in the library, the paintings in the galleries, and all manner of to-ings and fro-ings of staff and servants that constituted a great house in the country. Lindisfarne was all this and more, and it fairly took her breath away.

They were four days in advance of the wedding party, and they had travelled with Mr Drake who also would begin organizing the household to receive its mistress—and ultimately its new master—and all their guests. Mrs Mudge had not yet had the occasion to meet Mr Drake, and was curious to observe the relations between him and her old friend as husband and wife, and to ascertain if all the various virtues Mrs Drake had extolled of her husband were in fact true. The several hours' journey to Lindisfarne, stopping once at an inn to rest the horses and take some refreshment, gave her ample time to assess his character, his mind, his manners and to her great surprise, an affability of communication far beyond what one might expect of an established butler, if indeed one expected affability or communication at all in that class of person.

"You must allow me to express my gratitude," Mr Drake addressed her smoothly, unexpectedly, as she and he found themselves alone together, for a moment, waiting in the inner courtyard of the inn where they had stopped on their way, and while Mrs Drake was occupied elsewhere.

At Chalk Farm

He was a tall man, although not nearly as tall as her Mr Mudge, but prepossessing in his own way, neatly dressed in somber, suitable black, with an overcoat carefully folded on the seat in the carriage, and an umbrella in his hand at all times when outside, prepared to shelter his wife and her friend from the slightest drop of rain, which had threatened all morning.

They stood side by side, facing outward, taking in the wet cobblestones and scurryings of stable boys and servants, so Mr Drake only had to lean his head slightly in her direction to be heard. "Mrs Drake has been so occupied with her vocation, as it were, that I have been, at times, concerned for her health." Mrs Mudge glanced slightly upward toward his broad face, unadorned by beard or mustache, but manly in its squareness, its regularity of feature and flat planes, duly masking, as a butler's face should do, any inward emotions of judgement or thought—nonetheless, an intelligent face, a face to trust with a confidence of a sort. "She has spoken often to me of the great relief and help you have been to her." He leaned his solemn head an inch closer to Mrs Mudge. "This particular occasion," he added, *sotto voce*, "I believe, would not have been possible for her to undertake alone."

She looked more fully at his face upon hearing this, but he had straightened up and was looking out sharply for their particular stable boy who was in fact leading the pair of horses and their carriage—one of Lady Bradeen's second carriages—toward them, now fully equipped again for travelling onward. It was as if he had not spoken, and did not require acknowledgement of his words to her, but Mrs Mudge took the compliment as it was meant, and felt both gratitude and renewed pride in the decision she had made a

At Chalk Farm

few months ago, to join Mrs Drake in her entrepreneurial venture.

They were welcomed to Lindisfarne by an upright but no means unfriendly housekeeper, a Mrs Darnell, and while Mr and Mrs Drake were shown to a small apartment below stairs, Mrs Mudge was guided by a comely, chatty maid to a room of her own, not quite in the attics with the other female servants, but in a kind of turret or small tower set off a staircase at a landing a half floor below the servants' floor. She had to hide the burst of delight that filled her heart when she stepped into the room—it was rounded in shape, with two windows that looked out onto the gardens on the south side of the great house. In it were neatly placed a small bed, a tall, narrow wardrobe, and a tiny desk with a chair, facing one of the windows. There were curtains at the windows of a medium blue, tied back with almost festive yellow ribbons. She had never in her life had a room of her own, and this one was beyond any possible expectation she might have dreamt in her imaginings of her time at Lindisfarne.

"Oh yes, Missus," said the maid, catching her glances around the room, "tis a mighty lovely room, this is, used to be for governess."

Mrs Mudge spoke her surprise before she thought. "I didn't think Lady Bradeen had any children," she said, and immediately wished she hadn't said it.

"Oh no, Missus," said the maid, shaking her head, "not her Ladyship as is, but her old Ladyship, Milord's first wife that was, there was a daughter back then." The girl put Mrs Mudge's small case on the bed. "Before my time, actually, but me mum was here then." She smiled and nodded at Mrs Mudge. "Anythink I can do for ye, just call for Lily, that's me."

At Chalk Farm

"Thank you very much, Lily, I appreciate your looking out for me." There was a moment's awkwardness as Mrs Mudge wondered if she were expected to find a penny to give the girl, but Lily just smiled, bobbed a quick curtsey and left the room. She sighed, realized she had been rather nervous about this, her first encounter, alone, with a servant who was ministering to her, but felt she had at least acquitted herself without shame.

Ten

The four days' head start they had been allowed was scarcely sufficient to accomplish the work needed to procure, transport and arrange all the flowers for the various events surrounding the wedding ceremony itself, which was to take place on the Friday, three days after the arrival of Lady Bradeen and Captain Everard on Tuesday. The honored guests who would be staying at Lindisfarne would be arriving, some on the Tuesday afternoon, others on the Wednesday; for the lesser guests, rooms had been reserved at the principal inn in the nearby village of Landeston.

Our Mrs Mudge, though working for all she was worth, found herself floating in a haze of golden light, both real and figurative. The suggestive reaches of the landscape, when she was outdoors, presented to her lively imagination—fed by the ha'penny romance novels she often read—the very portals and *allés* of amorous walks in sun-dappled arbors; the interiors of the great house even more so. In every room, large and small, she pictured *têtes-à-têtes* breathless in their intimacy and charming in every detail of velvet, silk, precious jewellery and satin roses atop slender slippers. So full was her imagination with all the stimulus

At Chalk Farm

of wealth and beauty and history around her, she scarcely felt the need of Captain Everard—nay, any man at all!—to focus the scene upon any particular emotion or relation. She thought not at all of Mr Mudge.

The arrival of the affianced couple brought with it a new kind of thrill for her nerves—she had yet to see Lady Bradeen, after all these months, and she had not encountered the Captain again after that first time in the drawing room in town. And now, to see them together at last—she knew not what to expect, either of them or of herself. Mrs Drake, of course, seemed supremely unaware of any perturbation in her junior partner's emotions, as naturally she should be. Our young woman had not taken her into her confidence about any feelings she had for or about either of the two personages they served, and of course Mrs Drake had no notion whatsoever of that exquisite, private late summer afternoon meeting in the Park between the Captain and the former telegraphist.

She and Mrs Drake were part of the formal assemblage of servants at the entrance to the mansion when the mistress arrived, though indeed, our two ladies, not quite being servants nor quite figuring as friends, stood to the rear and to one side, separated from the household staff and nearly hidden by a pair of potted palm trees just inside the wide double doors.

Mr Drake, as was his role, was prominent and in the lead, the first to welcome Lady Bradeen to her home, as she stepped from the carriage after Captain Everard, who turned to hold out his hand to assist her. A rippling wave of curtsies and bows spread through the assembled servants as her Ladyship moved up the steps, graciously nodding and smiling at her household. The Captain, our young woman could just see, had a rather fixed smile on his handsome

At Chalk Farm

face; he seemed ill at ease and nervous. But perhaps, she thought, her own inner tumult was somehow coloring her perception of him. He looked to be in good health, but nothing compared to her Ladyship, who positively bloomed forth like a just fully opened pink rose, gleaming with fresh dew and fragrant with desire and anticipation—the very portrait of a young bride.

It appeared for a moment as if the two floral ladies were to be overlooked altogether as Lady Bradeen swept into the enormous entrance hall and turned directly to the staircase, away from where Mrs Drake and her junior partner stood among the palms. But Captain Everard, turning in their direction to hand his cane and hat to a footman, caught sight of them.

"Ah!" he said, quite involuntarily. "There you are!"

Her Ladyship turned back at that, looking wonderingly at her paramour, then she, too, recognized Mrs Drake, who had taken a step forward at the Captain's words.

"Oh, Mrs Drake!" cried her Ladyship, extending a hand. "I didn't see you there!"

Mrs Drake touched her employer's hand lightly and bowed her head deferentially.

Our young woman had had ample time to determine that the Captain's exclamation had actually been sounded upon seeing her, not Mrs Drake, and that Lady Bradeen took it to be the latter, which she felt was just as well. She didn't want attention, especially in any relation at all to Captain Everard. She had in fact taken a step back when Mrs Drake took one forward, so she was all the more hidden by the voluminous branches of the palm trees, and it seemed clear that Lady Bradeen had failed to see her altogether, as she took Mrs Drake possessively by the arm and began to

At Chalk Farm

assail her with questions, walking toward the stairs as she did so.

The servants had cleared out, swiftly returning to their various duties and floors, and Mr Drake was still outside, superintending the footmen bringing in luggage and boxes, and talking to the coachmen about the hazards and details of their journey. Our young junior partner could see him, through the open door, as he competently managed half a dozen tasks at once; but her attention was all for Captain Everard who stood, not quite at his ease, a moment longer in the hall.

"I wasn't sure you would actually be here," he said, a tentative smile, possibly embarrassed, touching his lips. "How do you fare at Lindisfarne, Mrs Mudge?"

"Very well, sir," she said, feeling the color in her face rise slightly. "We have been very busy." It was all she could think of to say.

"Well," said the Captain, taking a step away, "I'm sure her Ladyship and…and I…are very grateful for all that you're doing." He turned to ascend the staircase, where his valet, she assumed it was, waited halfway up, carrying a small bag and a wooden box. He didn't look back.

"Yes, sir," she said faintly, and curtsied. It wouldn't do for anyone, servant or guest, to see that she was in any way acquainted with, or even affected by, Captain Everard. She would have to watch herself, as he clearly was. But then, she thought, would there actually be any occasions when he and she would be permitted to converse or even exchange more than the most pedestrian pleasantries? She had to admit it was unlikely—unless, in the reaches of the night, perhaps, out on the lawn, or under the trees…. She shook herself to dismiss such thoughts, and hurried back into the dining room to make sure every flower and decorative touch she had labored on all morning would be perfect for the initiating dinner that night.

Eleven

The next morning brought further consultations between Mrs Drake and Lady Bradeen, with our Mrs Mudge set to rearranging and re-purposing the flowers from the previous night's dinner ("exquisite!" "perfect beyond saying!" were her Ladyship's exclamations, relayed by a buoyant Mrs Drake) for that day's luncheon. She was in the dining room, surrounded by bags of ribands, boxes of wires and sticks for binding, and large pots of flowers soaking their stems in water, patiently awaiting arrangement. Less patient were two under-footmen assigned to give her whatever assistance she needed, especially in lifting and placing the heavy crystal or ceramic vases and managing ponderous palm fronds and other large pieces of greenery.

"Oy, Missus, look at me!" cried the younger of the two, a boy scarcely in his teens. He had taken up an orchid that had fallen to the floor, and tucked the stem over his ear, striking a pose like a dancing girl and giggling. Mrs Mudge was suddenly, sharply, reminded of her poor, dead brother—he'd been about that age when he died of fever—and she felt a pang and a sudden affection for the clowning boy. But she knew her place, and knew she had to keep it, so she frowned and snapped at him.

"Here, give me that flower, boy!" she said, holding out her hand. "And carefully! Do you have any idea how much a flower like that costs?"

At Chalk Farm

"No, Missus," he said, sheepish now and grumbling as he handed over the stem.

"Well, more than you can imagine," she said, softening a little. "Go on, you both, bring that box over here, the one by the window with all the little statues in it." She watched as they trudged across the room, whispering to each other, and punching at each other's arms, stifling their laughter. They brought over the box and laid it at her feet. The older boy pointed to one of the statuettes.

"What's this?" he asked. "Why is the man kneeling?"

Mrs Mudge smiled and picked up the statue, then its mate, a woman, seated, with her fan partly covering her face. "These two belong together," she explained. "It's called a 'courting couple', you see, he's kneeling down asking her to marry him, and she's…well, she's thinking about it."

"On account of 'er Ladyship and the Captain's going to be married, I get it," said the boy.

"Right you are," said Mrs Mudge, smiling at him. She had only a moment to realize, with a start, how her affections seemed engaged by these two boys—she felt positively maternal—when Mrs Drake appeared at the door, all aflutter, and drew her attention away.

"The most unaccountable thing!" cried Mrs Drake, shooing away the two young under-footmen and closing the door as soon as they had left. "You'll never imagine, my dear!"

Mrs Mudge continued calmly to lift the statuettes from the box to the table; she had become used to Mrs Drake's flustered aggrandizements of simple situations. But she lifted her head and raised her brows in a questioning way.

At Chalk Farm

Mrs Drake pulled out a dining chair and sat on it without ceremony; then leaning close, and in a whisper, she relayed the dreadful news.

"Lord Bradeen's daughter has sent her Ladyship a note, saying she is coming here to visit—this week—today!" She looked intently at her young friend. "Surely she must know—only that she clearly doesn't—or doesn't care!—about the wedding!"

"Goodness," said Mrs Mudge, setting down a statuette with great care. "I can't even think…that is, I didn't even know there was such a daughter in question—she must be, well, she must be well into middle-age by now, don't you think?" She sat on a chair herself, facing Mrs Drake. She remembered what the maid had said about "a daughter, then" and realized she had assumed that the girl had probably died.

"I daresay, my dear, but it doesn't matter what age she is," said Mrs Mudge, with some asperity. "The idea of her coming here, of all times, when she has, you know, hardly given Lady Bradeen the time of day since her father married her, *our* Lady Bradeen I mean."

"Lady Bradeen is, I think, young enough to be *this* lady's daughter," mused Mrs Mudge. "Therein may lie the animosity, don't you think?"

"Well, yes, there's that," admitted Mrs Drake. She waved her hand in dismissal. "I'm sure that there may have been some, some uncomfortableness, at first, when it seemed there would likely be an heir—a *male* heir—to supplant Lydia Bradeen, for that's her name, you know, Lydia, only she's not Bradeen any longer, she has married, a Viscount D'arcy, I believe the name is. Irish, I think, but no matter. Anyway, as you know, there were no children for our Ladyship, but of course Viscountess D'arcy must feel

At Chalk Farm

it her right to be able to visit the house of her family when she wants to."

"Was this house left to *our*, as you say, Ladyship? Was there no provision for Lord Bradeen's only daughter?"

"Oh, well, I don't know about all those details," said Mrs Drake. "But the fact that she—Lady Bradeen—is *here*, that *we* are here doing what we're doing, says to me that this house belongs to Lady Bradeen."

Mrs Mudge nodded her head. It seemed likely, but one never knew. "But then this Viscountess is coming here, out of the blue, so that might be a sign…?"

Mrs Drake shook her head. "All I know is that it's got her Ladyship in a terrible state, she seems to see it as the ruin of all her wedding plans, and destroying every comfort and delight we have so worked on!"

"But surely the wedding won't be put off," Mrs Mudge tried to assure her partner. "After all, they are legally allowed to be married, even if it's a little soon for society's judgement, after Lord Bradeen's death last autumn."

"Horrors!" said Mrs Drake, drawing herself up. "I hadn't thought that far! Oh," she cried, "oh, I do hope they are not thinking of *that*!" She looked around the dining room, as if suddenly aware of the state it was in. "Heavens!" she said, looking at a little watch pinned to her breast. "This room is in no shape for luncheon, there's barely two hours before the guests will be seated!" She jumped up and started moving statues here and there haphazardly.

"Dear Mrs Drake, do let me take care of this," said Mrs Mudge, aware that she, on her own, was perfectly capable of putting the room together in the time left. Mrs Drake would only be a distraction. "Perhaps you should go to Lady Bradeen and see if there are changes coming that will affect what we are doing. I can manage this—please, the luncheon table will be just fine."

Mrs Drake drew a shaky breath, and pressed her young friend's shoulder with a trembling hand. "Thank you, my dear," she said. "I think you are quite right." She took another deep breath, and squared her shoulders. "It's quite too dreadful, though, quite!" She left the room swiftly, and Mrs Mudge returned to her task with renewed vigor, eager both to get the work done and to be left to herself to imagine the consequences of this dramatic, sudden visit.

Twelve

Of course it was not to be expected that either Mrs Drake or Mrs Mudge would be privileged to actually be introduced to Viscountess Lydia D'arcy, who came alone, that is, without the Viscount, although attended by her personal lady's maid and several other servants, male and female. Mrs Darnell, the housekeeper, was a bit put to it to find rooms for them all, but with a little shifting here and there, and doubling up, and putting some of the younger footmen in the stable rooms, all were accommodated. No one had any idea how long the Viscountess meant to stay nor, by all accounts heard below stairs, whether she actually knew the wedding was about to take place in two days or not.

Our two consulting florists, as a consequence of the continually arriving, exalted visitors upstairs, spent more of their time below stairs, especially for meals, and were obliged to hear, second-hand, what information could be derived from the overheard snatches of conversations in the dining room, the drawing room, even the hallways of the great house. The servants were, understandably, agitated

At Chalk Farm

and thrilled in equal measure by the dramatic possibilities inherent in this untimely visit by the late Lord's daughter to the late Lord's widow at such a juncture, and all of them, from the youngest chambermaid to the first footman, brought back fresh details and speculations on an hourly basis.

"Our Ladyship looked so pale, she did! Like as she couldn't 'ardly stand up, when first the Viscountess came in the drawin' room," reported a maid who had helped with the tea service.

"And then, when the Captain, when 'e walked in, that old cat looked to eat 'im alive right there," said a very young footman, his epithet promptly inviting a light cuff to the back of his head by a not very much older footman. He shook his head. "I was glad to be outa there right quick."

Not long after the Viscountess D'arcy had arrived, her personal maid appeared in the kitchen to consult with the cook about her lady's particular nutritional likes and dislikes. It happened that, at the same time, Mrs Mudge was seated at the far end of the servants' table, looking over sketches she had made of some flower arrangements for the chapel—the wedding was to take place in the family's private chapel, on one end of the endlessly long mansion; it was to be the most attention that had been paid the chapel in the last fifty years. She looked up when the lady's maid came to stand in the doorway, looking slowly around and then fixing on the rotund person of the cook, who was looking for a recipe in a big box on the table, her back to the door. There was no one but the two of them in the room, therefore discerning which one was the cook was hardly at issue. The lady's maid had barely looked at Mrs Mudge, thus confirming her initial perception that contempt and condescension were paramount in that person's attitude.

At Chalk Farm

"You are the cook?" said the lady's maid, addressing the woman at the recipe box.

"Why, goodness," said the cook, looking about her, "it appears that I am." She was one who brooked no nonsense from anyone, but had a fierce and understated sense of humor that Mrs Mudge had come to appreciate.

The lady's maid stepped further into the kitchen, looking as if she feared she might soil her fine clothing if she moved too quickly or came in too far. She took a piece of paper from her pocket, and holding out her hand, placed it on the table and shoved it toward the cook. In that moment, with that gesture—one of which our Mrs Mudge had been the recipient thousands of times during her years at Cocker's—she recognized, with a start, the lady's maid as one who had sent many dozens of telegrams from Cocker's, the majority of which Mrs Mudge had herself counted out and sent over the sounder. Her retentive mind, which had served her so well during the harrowing time of the scandal that had threatened Captain Everard and Lady Bradeen, drew forth words, then phrases, then whole telegrams that had been sent by this woman—on behalf of someone (coded to be sure) named "Purple," one of the oddest of all the code names our former telegraphist had seen, and therefore to which she had paid close attention.

She tucked away this information for the moment, and returned her attention to scrutinizing the Vicountess's lady's maid, who was busy condescending to the cook, and missing half the sarcasms with which the cook answered her. She was certainly elegantly dressed, as befitted a viscountess's personal maid, but the colors were subdued, puce and grey, and she wore no jewellery. Her face, though rather pretty, showed the lines of strain that, Mrs Mudge surmised, came from tightly controlled frustration and the

At Chalk Farm

lack of a certain kind of personal freedom—attributes which our young florist could sympathize with, particularly in having attained a situation where those feelings had less relevance for her than they'd had at Cocker's. It seemed to her that it was likely the Viscountess was a difficult woman to work for.

She doubted if the lady's maid would recognize her, much as Lady Bradeen had failed to see in Mrs Mudge the faceless (to her) civil servant at the post office who did her public duty in relative anonymity to the hundreds and thousands of the members of the public who formed the unceasing waves of customers requiring stamps, telegrams, information or maps. It took such a one as Captain Everard—and here she smiled inwardly, remembering—to look up and actually *into* the face on the other side of the bars, to see a person there, to see *her* there, as she was, at that time. Mrs Mudge gave a little sigh, and tried to brush away the thoughts. But she kept her face somewhat averted from the two women at the other end of the table, whose colloquy was coming to a close, as a precaution against any possible discovery. Not that it would matter, would it? But she felt somehow it was best to remain unknown.

The lady's maid was now practically scowling at the cook, who was looking up (she was rather short) with insouciant glee. "No such thing in my kitchen, madam," she was saying, with a great deal of satisfaction, Mrs Mudge thought. "I'm afraid you'll have to do with arrowroot at best, which is no mean thing, all in all."

The lady's maid did not deign to answer, and straightened up with disdain. "You seem to forget exactly to whose household you belong," she said severely. "Your attitude will be remembered." And so saying, she swept from the room, her chin in the air.

The cook laughed her out the door, and turning back to her recipe box, she glanced at Mrs Mudge and winked. Our young woman took the opportunity of the sudden shared moment.

"What do you suppose she meant by that?" she said to the cook. "Is it possible that Lady Bradeen is not in full possession of this house?"

The cook shook her head, her attention back on her recipes. "That's nought for the likes of me to know anything about, Missus," she said. "Them upstairs will have that sorted, I'm sure."

She looked up again at Mrs Mudge, and winked once more. "Every house needs a cook, to be sure," she said. "I have no fear of losing my place."

Mrs Mudge smiled, and returned to looking at her drawings. But her mind was very busy.

Thirteen

After dinner, when the guests and their hosts were in the drawing room with sherry and coffee, Mrs Drake came upstairs to find Mrs Mudge and consult with her about the latest plans and perturbations.

"Oh, my dear," she said, after her young friend had let her into the small room and raised the lamp light to make it easier to see each other. Mrs Drake was directed to sit in the small desk chair while Mrs Mudge perched on the end of the bed. Outside, the evening had turned to full dark, but the windows slightly open to the cool night let in the sounds of birds settling, the occasional lowing of cattle, and shouts from the stable yard. Mrs Mudge thought she had never lived in a pleasanter place—and probably never would again.

"Oh, my dear," Mrs Drake repeated, her hands tight in her lap. "Something very, very dreadful has occurred, I can hardly speak for the horror of it." Her lips were tightly compressed after this intriguing announcement, and Mrs Mudge leaned forward sympathetically, eager to hear, though somehow, less interested than she thought she should be.

She was beginning to feel that, after all, running about creating decorative *ambiances* for the pleasures of such people was at best a checkered pursuit, even if it paid well—after all, wouldn't she be rather more useful and perhaps, happier, doing for her own people—her husband, her mother—and herself? Although she did have some mixed feelings for the Captain, she felt with a sudden deep clarity that there was nothing in the fates and lives of these reckless aristocrats that could touch her very nearly, certainly not in the way that Mrs Drake manifested. She felt, with a jolt of self-knowledge, and then some amusement, that she, after all, belonged to Chalk Farm and Mr Mudge, and as mistress of both, had a place there which *meant* something, which could receive the stamp of her own personality. No scandal would threaten her overthrow there.

She saw that Mrs Drake was looking at her wonderingly, suspiciously, as if she had somehow caught the nature of her wayward, unloyal thoughts. She brought her attention back to her distressed friend.

"What is it, Mrs Drake?" she said. "Please do not keep me in suspense."

"Lady Bradeen, poor woman," Mrs Drake said, dabbing her eyes with a handkerchief, and a smidgeon of self-importance. "She is devastated, and yet, she keeps herself together with such fortitude!" She shook her head.

At Chalk Farm

"What is it that has happened?" Mrs Mudge persisted. She thought of the Viscountess's maid and the insinuations about the ownership of Lindisfarne. "Has the Viscountess come to claim the estate as her own?"

Mrs Drake twisted her handkerchief unmercifully, and tried to compose herself.

"All I know," she admitted, "is that there has been a…a discussion, and then a confrontation—perhaps even a threat! between the two ladies." She sniffed pitifully. "And that Lady Bradeen has talked of calling off the wedding…and then she turns around and says it will go forward no matter what ensues…I do not know what she means to do!" She practically wailed the last words.

Mrs Mudge frowned. "And what does the Captain say—what does he do?" she asked.

Mrs Drake unfurled her handkerchief and waved it about. "He is silent, silent! He is more stricken than she!" she said. "I take it to be his sense of honor, that it is all his fault, the trouble they're in—because of that bad, bad thing he did—that which she saved him from, you recall."

Mrs Mudge did recall, in detail, though only from the hints and obscurities that decorated the conversation with Mrs Drake at the end of the previous year, when she had learned that version of the story—that Lady Bradeen had "found" what was "lost" and thereby saved the Captain, and themselves, from scandal over the "very bad thing" he had done.

She knew to a certainty what she, herself, had done; what aid she had given—the wrong words in a single telegram, resurrected, which made everything all right. Could there have been something else, some *thing* that happened after her part in it?

At Chalk Farm

"Perhaps, whatever it was that had been previously lost, has become lost again?" she ventured, not without a sly tinge of seeming innocence. "Perhaps the Viscountess knows something about…the original scandal, and has threatened to expose them if Lady Bradeen does not give up the estate?" She pondered her own words even as she spoke. Somehow, with this appearance of his daughter, her thoughts flew to a possible connection to the untimely—or timely—death of Lord Bradeen. Could it be? Her eyes widened as the thought came home to her. Could they—could *he,* her Captain—in some way, be involved in that sudden death? Impossible! She shook her head at the thought. She would not believe it of the Captain—and how could a beautiful, charming woman like Lady Bradeen be brought to…? No, it was impossible.

"I don't know, my dear, I don't know," lamented Mrs Drake.

"What does Mr Drake say about all this?" asked our heroine.

"He is very circumspect," said Mrs Drake firmly. "Just as he should be. He says leave it to *her*—and to *him*—to sort it out. I daren't talk to him about it as I do to you, my dear."

Mrs Mudge received this in silence. An idea was forming in her head, but she must speak with the Captain, alone, and soon! She looked at the sagging form of her partner and friend, and felt she must comfort her.

"I agree with Mr Drake," she said, reaching over with a soothing hand on her friend's arm. "They will sort it out—they have resources—they know what they're about, don't they?" She tried to smile cheeringly. "It's not for us to solve their problems, you know," she said, adding silently to herself, *especially those they've made themselves.*

At Chalk Farm

Mrs Drake made some sounds of having been persuaded, and rose to leave the room. The two friends parted with a kiss on the cheek, and as Mrs Mudge closed the door and turned down the light, a scheme was hatching in her brain, one she knew she had to bring to fulfillment that very night.

Fourteen

It was long past midnight when our young woman heard the last servant climb the steps past her door and retreat to bed. Looking out her lovely windows in the round room, however, she could see the gas lamps in the drawing room were still lit, and could very faintly see the form of a gentleman on the back terrace, smoking. She was sure it was the Captain—she would know him anywhere, in darkness or fog—the way he held his cigar, the way he stood, straight and yet softly bending, moving with grace.

She was still dressed, and wrapped a dark shawl around her shoulders. She meant to quietly go down to the conservatory, which abutted the back terrace—if anyone saw her there, she could quite satisfactorily explain she was checking on some of the plants and flowers there that were to be moved to the chapel the next day—in fact, she felt she ought to do that, as Mrs Drake seemed so preoccupied with possible disaster, the details might be escaping her.

She made her way down the stairs into the main hall via a green baize door, carrying a small candle in a glass and hammered tin lantern, to keep it from going out, and walked swiftly across the hall, through the smaller drawing room, now empty entirely, and into the conservatory. The larger drawing room, outside which Captain Everard stood

At Chalk Farm

smoking, flanked the other side of the conservatory. As she moved across the stone floor, hearing the drip of water from the pots, and the hum of a nighttime insect in the upper reaches of the glass structure, she could see him through the slightly misted windows. She made haste, soundlessly—she might never have another such opportunity to speak with him. Nearing the glass door that gave onto the terrace, and shielding her light a little, she cautiously opened the door—it creaked and, like that day some months ago when she had surprised the Captain in London at Lady Bradeen's townhouse, he turned toward her at the sound.

"Is someone there?" he said, softly. He took a step or two closer, and Mrs Mudge held up her light to show her face.

"It's you," he said, and what seemed to her to be a grateful smile broke the former gloom of his face.

"Yes, it is I," she said, smiling back. She felt she could stay in this moment forever.

They stood face to face and then, mindful of their location, our young woman stepped back, and motioned to him to come inside with her. She did not want to be overheard.

The Captain closed the glass door behind him, after tossing his cigar out onto the lawn, and the warm, humid air, redolent of soil and the fragrances of many blooms, curled around them. Our young woman placed her candle-lantern carefully on a small table.

"I have heard," she began, "I have been told—and have heard in the chatter below stairs—that there is a serious...situation...unfolding between Lady Bradeen and Lord Bradeen's daughter, the Viscountess." She was, amazingly to herself, calm and detached. There was none of the cheekiness of her encounter, at the cage at Cocker's, with

At Chalk Farm

Captain Everard at his moment of greatest need, when she took on the persona of the telegraphist with the flute-like accent of Paddington, when she turned to him the maddening, blank face of the petty civil servant, playing with him with as little mercy as a rook with a worm. But it was different now—she was different.

Captain Everard looked at her, amazed himself. And smiled, rueful. "Yes, word does get about in these great houses, of course." Then he looked suddenly wary. "What have you to do with it?" It was gently said, and our young woman did not feel it as an insult. After all, how *could* he think she would have anything to do with it at all?

She felt the time rushing away, and decided there was no need for elaborate explanations. He would take it from her, or not, just as he pleased.

"Tell me," she said, "is it true there is a threat—to you, to Lady Bradeen—coming from the Viscountess?"

He looked even more surprised, hesitated a moment, then almost shrugged. "You always were—and are—a sharp observer," he said simply. He folded his arms across his chest, almost a defiance. "Yes," he said simply.

"And has this something to do with the scandal that so nearly overwhelmed you both late last year, and"—she hesitated a moment, but kept going—"with the sudden death of Lord Bradeen?"

"Yes," he said. But a hard look had come into his eyes, and she felt a chill run through her. It came to her that he could, with that look in his eyes, actually could have, perhaps, done murder.

"I never mean to mention it again, ever," she said, gathering a confidence from inside herself that, somehow, reminded her of her husband's calm dealing with the

At Chalk Farm

drunken man at Cocker's. "Not to you or anyone else, because I think there is a way out of your present dilemma that will—as they say—put paid to it."

She watched his face change through three or four emotions, change color from pale to red, and then, composed, he dropped his eyes.

"You must trust me, you see," she said, and he raised his eyes to her, and nodded his head.

She could see, all at once, that he felt himself to be in her hands. She was completely in charge. The exhilaration was almost too much for her to bear without bursting into song, or laughter, or tears. She would be able to finish this, once and for all—she felt she owed it to him, and to herself.

"I will give you the key to stop the Viscountess," she said, and watched his face change from wonder to wonder—at those words, at their meaning, at her.

"You have simply to say to her, or have Lady Bradeen say to her, one word," she said. She hung fire another moment, savoring, despite herself and her good intentions, the power she had at that moment.

"Purple," she said.

"Purple?" he repeated.

"Trust me," she said. "The Viscountess will go away."

His look then was exceedingly hard to read. "Purple," he said again. Then he started to laugh. "You know her name is Lydia?"

Our Mrs Mudge was caught at this, nonplussed. She nodded, and looked her question.

"Lydia is Greek for purple," he said, laughing some more.

"Oh!" Mrs Mudge was struck, both at the silliness of it and the fact that it proved she was right.

At Chalk Farm

Captain Everard grasped her hand in both of his and bestowed a long kiss on the back of it. "I trust you," he said. "You said you would do..."

"Everything! Anything! For you, yes, I know," she said, laughing at last, though struggling not to cry out in her triumph.

After a moment she withdrew her hand, picked up her lantern, and made her way through the silent house back to the room in the tower.

Fifteen

The Viscountess departed before luncheon the next day, and the liveliness and high spirits of the wedding party rose to near hysteria, judging from the shrieks of laughter from the drawing room and the orders for bottle after bottle of champagne, at luncheon and for some time thereafter. At five o'clock, however, the house was silent, with guests dispersed about the grounds or in their rooms, and Lady Bradeen retired to her bridal chamber, not even to appear at dinner, to prepare for the wedding the next morning.

Mrs Mudge was aware that the couple, as soon as the wedding luncheon was over, were departing for Europe—for Paris and Rome and points beyond. By late afternoon, today, Thursday, the chapel was complete for the ceremony, and the luncheon table was already arranged. She found, a little to her surprise, that she wasn't much interested in attending the wedding, placed, as she would be, in the back with the rest of the household staff. She stood now in the grand entranceway, a basket of greens in her hand, and looked around her at the grandeur of Lindisfarne—its halls, its staircases, its gardens and lawns—and gave a little

At Chalk Farm

sigh of pleasure, a small smile of regret, and then a larger sigh of relief. If only she could go home—home! Chalk Farm, home?—yes, if only she could go home now and leave all this behind her. It was a dream, in many ways, but she was a practical woman, and didn't want to live in someone else's dream.

A footman broke her reveries, coming up to her with due respect, and handed her a little pale pink envelope. Her eyes brightened—it was a telegram! She, the counter of words and sender of telegrams for countless others—she was the recipient of a telegram all to herself. She thanked the boy and moved to sit down on a stately chair along the wall. There was no one there but herself, no one to notice or chide or take offense at this liberty. She set down the basket of greenery, and carefully opening the envelope, took out the so very thin piece of paper with its black telegraphic markings. It read:

```
          Caroline Mudge,
    c/o Lindisfarne House, Landeston

Shall come to bring you home Friday STOP
Ready by ten am STOP If not, will stay
til you are ready STOP Robert Mudge END
```

Oh, my dear, thought our young woman, *I am ready. I am so very ready.*

She carefully read the telegram again, realized she was counting up the words and the cost, then folded it, put it back into the envelope, and sat with a smile on her face for a very long time.

Excerpt from
Portraits of an Artist: A Novel about John Singer Sargent
by Mary F. Burns

Featuring Henry James

I rang the doorbell to John Sargent's studio promptly at a quarter to eight o'clock that evening, and stood a few steps back. I remember I was dressed for the cool rainy night in a suit of dark grey and a soft hat, and I carried an umbrella. John quickly descended the stairs to greet me personally, as I had imagined he would. I bent my head in a brief salutation as he opened wide the heavy door.

"Good evening, my dear Mr. James," he said, and held out his hand, American style. Although my grip was firm enough, John, I could see, recalled at the last instant that I had complained to him of "the crushing handshakes of our fellow Americans," and he lightened his own grasp accordingly.

We climbed the steps slowly to accommodate my somewhat elderly pace—though I was not yet forty at that time, I know I appeared to John's eyes to hover closer to his father's generation than his own. He maintained a convivial silence, turning to smile encouragingly at the landing, courteously allowing me to catch my breath until we reached the second floor.

The lamps were lighted to chase away the winter shadows, and a fire was burning briskly on the hearth. He had foreseen the need for a *remontant*, and led me to sit at a small table near the windows overlooking the street below. He poured some sherry into glasses and after a few sips, I was able to look about me as I regained my breath.

"What a lovely space you have here, Mr. Sargent," I said, gazing around keenly. "How happy you must be in your creations, here, above the fray and bustle of the streets below."

"Thank you," he said. He topped off our glasses, and sat down, facing the window. We gazed out at the twinkling lights of the city. Our silence was not awkward, but not yet quite easy.

"You, too, must have such a retreat," he said after a few moments. "A writer's study, all brown and dim and crammed with books, yes?"

I inclined my head and smiled. "Do you see that in your painter's eye?" He turned and looked at me, critically, as if sizing me up as a subject.

"Someday, I shall paint you, shall I, Mr. James?" he said.

An odd thought crossed my mind, but I took care not to let it cross my face. I smiled again. "Our Puritan forebears would no doubt consider it frivolous idolatry," I said, and sipped more sherry.

John laughed, a short bark of jollity that acknowledged in a moment our common Boston background and all the weight of its heritage on our expatriate shoulders. Yes, he was as I had thought—pure American youth, and yet there was the uncanny *savoir faire* of Europe in his face, almost a frightened weariness, at times.

We sat for several moments more, growing more comfortable with each other. I roused myself, now recovered from the labor of mounting the stairs, and began to stroll about the room, looking at the portraits arranged carefully as for exhibition. John continued in his chair, watching with amusement as I leaned into, and stepped back from, the various works on display.

"I saw, last year in London," I said, my voice echoing slightly in the high-ceilinged room, "your splendid 'Doctor Pozzi' at the Academy. Did you know that he had been placed in the same room as the two Cardinals?" I turned an inquisitive eye to him, and he shook his head. "Ah, you should have seen it," I said. "Millais' 'Cardinal

Newman', a very holy man and a very superior model," I continued, peering closely at a portrait of Albert de Belleroche, whom I knew but slightly, "though unfortunately dressed in a garment of a very furious red, painted with a crudity which caused it to obliterate the face, but without justifying itself. It is violent, monotonous, superficial, uninteresting; it is nothing but a cape, and yet it is not even a cape."

I could see he was amused at my studied manner in relaying my criticism of the exhibition—I presume he knew I wrote critiques for the London journals—and he let me comment without interruption.

"The Cardinals have had poor luck this past year," I continued, "Cardinal Manning having been sacrificed simultaneously to Mr. Watts, whose effort is less violent than that of Mr. Millais, but not more successful." I sighed, and turned to the portrait of Madame Gautreau. I had heard much about it from John's friends in the past days. I looked it up and down, but moved on after a moment, and continued where I left off.

"The best that can be said of Mr. Watt's portrait of Cardinal Manning is that it is not so bad as his portrait, at the Grosvenor, of the Prince of Wales, of which I shall say no more, as I fear it would expose the artist to the penalties attached to that misdemeanor known to English law as 'threatening the Royal Family.'"

John laughed aloud at this sally, poured himself another sherry, and brought another full glass to me.

"But your flamboyant physician," I said, taking the glass and lifting it in salute, "out-Richelieus the English Cardinals, and is simply magnificent."

He bowed his thanks, and smiled mischievously. "Do you know what he is called, here in Paris, by his patients?"

I shook my head, raising an eyebrow.

"*Le Docteur Amour*," he said, laughing.

"Indeed," I said, and took another sip of sherry. "Doctor Love. Well."

"Did you see my Venetian studies, at the Grosvenor?" he asked, obviously feeling more comfortable.

"Yes, most wonderful," I said. "I thought the figures of the women, sitting in gossip over some humble, domestic task in the big, dim hall of a shabby old palazzo, were extraordinarily natural and vividly portrayed."

I pondered those paintings in my mind; they made me feel wistful. "You have seen and captured that part of Venice," I said, "which the tourist does not know, and which only such as you and I, wandering the narrow walks in the shadows, have the heart and the sensibility to observe, and to love, observing."

"Yes," John said, softly. "Thank you for saying it so well, I never—have the words—" His voice trailed off, and he walked away to restore the glasses to the little table by the window. I remained standing before the portrait of a gondolier, gazing down at the sharp and feral face, and with what I trusted was an impenetrable look on my own.

"Shall we go to dinner then?" John said, returning and glancing at his watch. He added in a kindly, though jocular tone, "Going down the staircase will be much easier than coming up!"

I smiled faintly, and bowed my head. "Seeing you, in your studio, is worth any number of stairs, my dear Mr. Sargent."

Praise for *Portraits of an Artist*

෨

"An evocative rendering of the great portraitist, John Singer Sargent, as seen through the eyes of the subjects of his most famous paintings. A *tour de force* of historical and psychological imagination."
 —Paula Marantz Cohen, *What Alice Knew, Jane Austen in Scarsdale*

෨

"Set in the Europe of 1882, the writing is richly subtle and each character exquisitely drawn. One hears murmurs behind doors and the truth just beyond the corner until the hearts of two women—one very young and one very beautiful—are broken forever. In the end of this fascinating novel, however, it is the portrait of the young artist himself, still an enigma, which lingers in the reader's mind. Wonderful writing!" —Stephanie Cowell, *Claude & Camille, Marrying Mozart, The Players: A Novel of the Young Shakespeare*

෨

Other Books by Mary F. Burns

The Spoils of Avalon

The first mystery in a new series introduces two life-long friends as a different kind of detecting team: the brilliant and brittle Violet Paget (writing as Vernon Lee), and the talented, genial portrait painter John Singer Sargent. The death of a humble clergyman in 1877 leads the amateur sleuths into a medieval world of saints and kings as they follow a trail of relics lost since the destruction of Glastonbury Abbey in 1539.

The Love for Three Oranges

This second mystery finds John Sargent and Violet Paget afloat in murder in the fabled City of Venice during the darkest days of the year. Dark secrets and long-held grudges surface at Ca' Favretto, an ancient palazzo on the Grand Canal, where the ghosts of the past collide with the passions of the present, resulting in murder and tragedy.

J-The Woman Who Wrote the Bible

Like the women of the Red Tent, even the daughter of King David lived in a world ruled by men. But this woman was born to break the rules of both men and God in order to learn the art of writing, and with it, a power that could reveal the hidden truth, or slay a man with a single word.

Ember Days

On the edge of the cultural earthquake that would be the 1960s, the tiny coastal village of Mendocino can feel it coming. Beat poetry, jazz, rebellion and art are spilling out of San Francisco onto the northern coasts of California. World War II is laid to rest, but people feel restless. When a village son, now a priest, comes home to bury his mother, he finds his younger brother gone and a town full of secrets—some of them his own.

Mary F, Burns was born in Chicago, Illinois and attended Northern Illinois University in DeKalb, where she earned both Bachelors and Masters degrees in English. She relocated to San Francisco in 1976 where she now lives with her husband. Ms. Burns has a law degree from Golden Gate University. She is a member of and book reviewer for the Historical Novel Society and a former member of the HNS Conference board of directors; a member of the Henry James Society, and a contributor to Tiferet Journal. She has presented papers at the Sargentology Conference at the University of York, England (2017), and at the Henry James Society annual conference in Trieste, Italy (2019).

Ms. Burns may be contacted at maryfburns@att.net.
Visit the author's website at www.maryfburns.com.

Printed in Great Britain
by Amazon